THE CLUE OF THE BROKEN BLADE

FRANK and Joe Hardy become involved in an intriguing mystery which revolves around their fencing master, Ettore Russo. Proof that Russo is the rightful heir to his grandfather's estate hinges on retrieving the guard end of a broken saber lost many years ago in California.

The young investigators' quest is complicated by a bank robbery during which some of their father's important records are stolen. Using Mr. Hardy's recently purchased scientific device, a sound spectrograph, the boys identify the voiceprints of the leader of the masked robbers. A chase ensues that takes Frank, Joe, and their pal Chet Morton to the grape-growing region of California and involves them in a dangerous game of hide-and-seek with the bank robbery gang, who also are searching for the broken saber.

A startling discovery at a movie location leads to the solution of this thrilling, fast-paced mystery.

Frank was pushed directly into the path of the motorcycle

The Hardy Boys Mystery Stories®

THE CLUE OF THE BROKEN BLADE

BY

FRANKLIN W. DIXON

GROSSET & DUNLAP
Publishers • New York
A member of The Putnam & Grosset Group

Published by Grosset & Dunlap, Inc., a member of The Putnam & Grosset Group, New York. Published simultaneously in Canada. Printed in the U.S.A.

Library of Congress Catalog Card Number: 73-119043 ISBN 0-448-08921-1
13-Digit: 978-0-448-08921-8
7 9 10 8 6

CONTENTS

THE CLUE OF
THE BROKEN BLADE

CHAPTER I

Foiled

FRANK and Joe Hardy, masked and gloved, confronted each other with crossed foils. Ettore Russo, the slim, erect fencing master, was coaching them. He seemed nervous.

"Frank, you attack. Joe, you parry. On guard. Bend your elbow a little bit more, Frank. Now thrust. Lunge!"

While Frank carried out the instructions, he murmured to himself, "Something's bothering Russo. He's not himself today."

"Look, Frank," came Russo's voice. "Thrust first until your arm is fully extended, then lunge. Okay. You can take a break now."

Dark-haired, eighteen-year-old Frank and his blond brother Joe, who was a year younger, removed their masks and gloves. They were about to join a group of friends when Russo called them aside.

"What's on your mind, maestro?" Frank asked as they walked up to him.

"I won't be here for the tournament," Russo said glumly.

Joe's eyebrows shot up. "How come?"

"My grandfather's will is being probated in Switzerland. I'll have to be there."

"Your grandfather just died?" Frank asked.

"No, many years ago. It's my step-grandmother who just died. She was in her eighties."

Russo smoothed his wiry black hair with his hand and continued, "You see, Granddad married a young girl late in life. In his will he left his fortune in trust, the income going to her during her lifetime. But the capital was to revert to his blood heirs after her death."

"And now you'll get an inheritance?" Joe asked.

"Maybe. My grandfather's will states that upon her death the estate is to be divided according to the terms specified on the sword Adalante."

"Now what does Adalante mean?" Joe wanted to know.

"Adalante is a championship saber that grandfather owned. Unfortunately it was broken and lost in a duel he had in California in the late eighteen hundreds. The tip end was found and is now in the possession of a cousin in Tessin, the Italian part of Switzerland. But there is no will etched on it, so it must be on the guard end."

"Do you think your grandfather was playing a joke?" Frank asked. "How could he expect anyone to find the other half of the broken blade?"

"He was eccentric all his life," the maestro said. "Maybe his idea was to test the ingenuity of his grandsons."

"Could be. Now what happens?"

"My grandfather often told my father that his first grandson would get three-fourths of the estate, the balance to be divided among his other grandchildren. I'm the eldest grandson."

"That's terrific!" Joe said.

Russo shrugged. "My father is no longer alive to testify. And my cousin Fabrizio Dente, based on a claim by his mother, who is still living, declares that he is the sole heir."

Frank shook his head. "It certainly leaves you in a fix. Unless you find the other end of the saber, of course."

Russo sighed. "Did you ever look for a needle in a haystack? All I can do is go to Switzerland and fight my cousin in court. That means I'll have to close the school."

The Hardys' friends, Biff Hooper, a blond six-footer, and olive-skinned Tony Prito, joined them.

"Close the school?" Biff said. "That means we can't take part in the tournament!"

Russo nodded sadly. "I've no one to replace me."

"We could keep the school open for you," Biff

offered. "We can't give lessons, but we can supervise training a few evenings a week!"

Frank grinned. "That's a good suggestion. We'll mind the store for you, maestro!"

Russo looked rather relieved. "Maybe it would work," he said. "I don't know when I'll be back, and if I close down too long, I might lose most of my students."

Phil Cohen and rotund Chet Morton, the Hardys' best pals, had joined the group and Chet spoke up. "Stop worrying, maestro. I'll pitch in, too. But I want a handicap from now on!"

Russo looked puzzled. "Why?"

"Well," Chet explained, "I've got a lot more surface to touch!"

Everyone laughed, and Biff needled Chet about his giant-sized appetite.

"We'll work the extra weight off you!" Russo promised. "Come on. You and Tony have a practice bout."

The two donned their wire-mesh masks and suede single gloves worn on the weapon hand. They took positions on the salle strip which was quite close to regulation size, six feet wide and forty feet long.

The maestro acted as bout director, taking his place about eight feet from the strip and halfway between Chet and Tony.

"Biff and Frank, start out by watching Chet," he said. "Phil and Joe, watch Tony."

Frank and Joe had studied the rules for fencing with foils, which were slightly different from those for épée and saber. In foil, the first to score a total of five touches was the winner. Touches were counted only if they were on the trunk of the body. Those on arms, legs, and head were off target. The latter incurred no penalty, but did not score, either.

If a contestant was hit, the judges would raise an arm and call out *hit* or *touch*.

The boys made a few lunges, bent the blades to the floor to test their flexibility, then saluted each other by raising the blades vertically in front of their masks.

"Ready?" the director said.

Tony and Chet assumed their guard positions, right foot forward, knees slightly bent, sword arm bent into a V, foils crossed and touching. Both boys answered, "Yes."

"Fence!" the director commanded.

Chet advanced, making a feint as he did. Tony retreated one pace, guessed that Chet's move was a feint rather than a real attack, thrust and lunged instead of parrying.

Biff and Frank raised their right arms and said, "Touch!"

"Halt!" the director ordered and called one against Chet.

The next two touches were off target, one off Chet's right shoulder, the other on Tony's left arm. Although they were not counted as penalties, the director halted the action each time, just as he did for good touches.

At the command "Fence!" Chet immediately moved to attack. Tony retreated, the blades clashing as lunge was met by parry, and parry by counterparry.

Chet scored the next two good touches, then Tony made three in a row. Chet took three more to win!

"Bout!" the director said. "Chet, you don't need a handicap!" He turned to Tony. "You failed to anchor your left foot when you made that last advance lunge. Next time hold it flat on the floor and you'll keep your balance if you're parried."

"Yes, sir," Tony said ruefully, "I'll remember."

The fencing lessons were one hour for each group. Frank and Joe got home in plenty of time for dinner. As they turned into the driveway, they saw a truck backed up to the stairway leading to their laboratory over the garage. Two men were unloading a large crate.

The boys got out of the car and went over to them. The wooden crate was about two feet square and more than two feet high. It was marked "Fragile."

"What's that?" Frank asked the men.

"Mr. Hardy ordered it," one of them replied. "He told us to put it in the lab."

Tony thrust and lunged

Frank and Joe looked at each other. Their father had been out of town for two weeks. As a famous private investigator Fenton Hardy had many enemies, and this would not be the first time someone had used a ruse to get into their expensive lab and damage it.

Joe asked, "What's in that crate?"

The man who had spoken shrugged. He and his colleague dragged the crate off the truck and began to carry it up the stairs. It looked as though it weighed well over a hundred pounds.

"Wait a minute!" Joe said, following them.

Frank ran after Joe. The men continued on, paying no attention to them. Then, halfway up, one of them missed a step.

The heavy crate teetered dangerously toward Joe!

CHAPTER II

Curious Strangers

JOE grabbed the man about the waist to steady him. At the same time Frank reached past his brother to catch a corner of the crate and keep it from falling. After a heart-stopping moment, the man recovered his footing.

From below a voice called up, "Careful there. That equipment's quite expensive!"

They all looked down. A taxicab was backing out of the driveway and Fenton Hardy, a suitcase in one hand and a small package in the other, stood at the bottom of the stairway.

Frank ran down. In a tone of relief he said, "Are we glad to see you, Dad! We didn't know if these deliverymen were on the level or not."

"They're only carrying out my instructions," Mr. Hardy replied. "I'll be back as soon as I take my suitcase inside. Meantime you can uncrate my new acquisition. But be careful. It's delicate."

By the time Fenton Hardy returned to the lab, the deliverymen had left in their truck and the boys had uncrated the object.

"This is a complicated piece of equipment," Joe remarked as they set it gently on the floor.

Four dials were on the front panel. Three were labeled *Monitor Level, Scan Playback Level,* and *Recording Level.* The fourth could be turned to any of three stops, which were marked *Mark Amp, Scan Plbk,* and *Rec Amp.* There were also four plug-in holes—*Scan Output, Line In, External Speaker,* and *Microphone Input.*

Joe wondered whether it was a special radio or a secret decoder.

"Neither," said Frank. "Look here." He pointed to a small, round speaker, a meter with a needle pointer, a pair of tape-recording spools, three rows of push buttons, and a drumlike contraption with heavy white paper rolled onto it.

Mr. Hardy came in, still carrying the small package.

"What is it, Dad?" Joe asked. "Some new outer-space device?"

His father set down the package and gave the machine a fond pat. "It's a sound spectrograph," he said. "The latest gadget to combat the world of crime."

"What does it do?" Frank wanted to know.

"It converts voices into picture patterns," Mr. Hardy explained, "and records them on that roll of paper in the form of graphs. It is based on the fact that no two persons have identical vocal cavities. That is what gives each person's voice its distinctive tone."

Joe said, "Couldn't a criminal beat it just by disguising his voice?"

Mr. Hardy shook his head. "The spectrograph can't be fooled. Experiments have been conducted with the best voice imitators in show business, and the device always instantly identifies them."

"What do you intend to use it for?" Frank asked.

Mr. Hardy opened the package. It contained several reels of sound tape. "I have collected recordings of the voices of top criminals in the country, and plan to make spectrograms of all of them and keep them on file. Just like fingerprint files are kept."

"Don't the various police departments have records like this?" Frank asked.

"Some do, with great success. In cases of kidnapping, for instance, the kidnapper's voice can be taped when he phones a ransom demand, and then be checked against the file."

"Say, that's great!" Joe exclaimed. "Will you show us how to use it?"

"I insist," Mr. Hardy said with a smile. The detective had tutored his sons in anti-crime technology ever since they had shown an interest in the subject. Fenton Hardy, his skills honed to a fine edge in the New York Police Department, had gained renown as a super sleuth. He left the force to set up a private practice, and when Frank and Joe grew old enough, they assisted him. Their first case was known as *The Tower Treasure,* and their latest success was called the *Mystery of the Flying Express.*

Both boys were eager to learn more about the sound spectrograph.

"Let's start right away!" Joe said.

"Take it easy," Mr. Hardy replied. "It's quite complicated. The manufacturer conducts a two-week training course in New Jersey. I'll phone to Somerville in the morning and arrange for you to attend."

Frank and Joe were enthusiastic.

"Incidentally," their father added, "by the time you come back from Voiceprint School, your mother and I won't be here."

"New case?" Frank asked.

"No. Just a plain old vacation. Don't you think we deserve one?"

Frank grinned. "Where are you going, Dad?"

"Grand Canyon. Aunt Gertrude will be here, however; so the house won't be empty when you return."

"Oh, don't worry about us, Dad. And have a good time," Joe said.

The Voiceprint Identification Course, as it was officially called, began the following Monday.

The boys arrived in Somerville on Sunday evening and registered at a motel next to the school.

When they reported to their first class at the Voiceprint Laboratories early the next morning, they learned that the course involved seventy hours of classroom lectures and laboratory work, plus twenty hours of homework.

"Looks as if we won't have much spare time," Joe said during lunch.

Frank nodded. "My head's spinning already with all the new info. They really cram it into your skull!"

The boys spent the next few days either in class or in the lab, and did not relax until evening when they had dinner in the motel's restaurant.

On Thursday night they called their father. He told them that he had completed the voiceprint records and stored them with the tapes in the Bayport Bank and Trust Company for safekeeping.

"That was a good idea," Frank said. "Especially since you won't be home for a while." He told his father of their progress, wished him a good trip, and hung up.

"Okay, let's get some chow," Joe suggested.

They had just settled themselves for dinner in the dining room, when two men entered and took a table next to their booth. One was tall, thin, and had a sad face, the other was burly with a swarthy complexion.

At the same time the boys heard someone slide into the booth next to theirs on the other side of the dividing partition.

After the waitress had taken their orders, the burly man smiled at Frank and said, "Evening, boys."

They politely returned the greeting.

"We've noticed you in here before," the man continued. "Are you staying at the motel?"

"Yes, sir," Joe said. "We're taking the Voiceprint Identification Course next door."

"Oh?" the man said. "I thought that was only for people in police work. Aren't you a little young for that?"

"Well, our Dad . . ." Joe started to reply when Frank kicked him under the table.

To Joe's relief the waitress interrupted the conversation by bringing the food. They all ate in silence for a few minutes.

Then the burly man said, "I'll bet those machines are quite expensive."

"Nearly fifteen thousand dollars," Frank said.

The thin man asked, "Can anyone buy them?"

Frank and Joe looked at each other. Were they being pumped? Had the two men followed them into the restaurant on purpose?

Even though he was suspicious, Frank decided there would be no harm in answering the thin man's question. He said, "The machines are sold chiefly to law-enforcement agencies and government offices. But a few have been purchased by private individuals. People who apply for machines are thoroughly investigated, however. If they are found to have any criminal connections, they're turned down."

The strangers asked no more questions. They finished eating before the Hardys, gave them polite good-bys, and left.

Frank said, "I think they were fishing for information, don't you?"

"Yes," Joe said. "But I wonder why. Do you think they are some kind of criminals?"

"I'm pretty sure of it. Did you see how they looked at each other when I told them anyone who wanted to buy a spectrograph was investigated? In the morning we had better warn the people at the Voiceprint Lab to take extra precautions against burglary."

"But why would criminals want a sound spectrograph?" Joe asked.

Frank shrugged. "I don't know. Anyway, it's a good thing you didn't spill the beans about Dad's project."

"Right," Joe said. "First time I've ever been thankful for a kick in the ankle."

They discussed Mr. Hardy's catalog system. "I'm glad he put it in the Bayport Bank and Trust Company," Frank said.

Just then they heard the sound of someone leaving the booth on the other side of the partition.

Suddenly realizing that whoever had been there had heard their conversation, the boys rose and peered over the top.

They could only see the man's back as he went out the door. He was broad-shouldered and thin-hipped, and wore a dark-blue suit. A black Homburg was perched on the back of his head.

As the Hardys sank back into their seats, Frank said, "I hope he wasn't a crook, too. We sure gave him an earful."

The boys were in bed by ten that night, but at three o'clock in the morning Joe suddenly sat up. He shook Frank and whispered, "Hey! I think I just heard a truck pull in behind the lab next door!"

Frank got up at once and put his trousers on over his pajamas. In less than a minute both boys were dressed and out of the motel room. Silently they moved toward the back of the Voiceprint Laboratories.

As they reached the corner of the building, they saw the outline of a truck. Even though it was a moonless night they could make out the figure of a man sneaking into the back entrance.

"Come on," Joe whispered. "Let's get him."

"Not yet."

"Why?"

"We don't know how many are inside. If there's a half dozen of them, they'll clobber us."

"Then I'll go for the police."

Frank put a hand on his brother's arm. "Look, they're coming out."

One man emerged slowly, walking out backwards and straining under a heavy load. Then a second figure came into sight. Between them they hefted a large crate.

"Hurry," one of them said hoarsely. "The wood's cutting into my fingers!"

"Shut up," came the reply. "What about me? My back's breaking!"

Frank whispered, "On your mark, Joe!"

CHAPTER III

The Legacy

THE men set the crate down, apparently to rest before lifting it onto the truck. As they stooped to pick it up again, Frank signaled Joe and the two moved forward.

"What are you doing here?" Frank called out.

The men dropped the crate and whirled. One swung a fist at Frank. The other leaped toward Joe.

Ducking, Frank drove a left, then a right into his attacker's stomach. The man doubled over with a gasp and his hat fell to the ground.

Meantime Joe and the other man were standing toe to toe, trading blows. In the darkness they could not see each other's faces. The man grunted when Joe landed a hard blow on his chest. But then he caught Joe in the middle of the forehead and knocked him down.

Frank was ready to finish off his man when he saw Joe fall. He turned to attack Joe's opponent, whereupon his adversary hit him from behind with a rabbit punch, driving Frank to his hands and knees.

"Let's get out of here!" the thug shouted.

Though dazed, Frank was aware of both truck doors being slammed shut. Then his head cleared and he looked up just as the vehicle started to pull away. The driver switched on his lights. This illuminated the rear license plate—New Jersey, FHB-548. Frank memorized it.

As he scrambled to his feet, Joe also got up. "Are you all right?" his brother asked.

"Okay," Frank mumbled. "How about you?"

"I'll live," Joe said, fingering a growing lump on his forehead.

Frank went over to look at the crate the thieves had left behind. Its label showed that it contained a sound spectrograph of the same model owned by their father.

Joe whistled. "Hey, one of those guys left his hat," he said, picking it up.

"Bring it along," Frank said. "We'll go back to the motel and call the police."

When they returned to their room, Joe exclaimed, "This is the same kind of hat as the one the man was wearing in the restaurant tonight!"

Frank took the black Homburg. He examined the inside. He lifted out a hair and studied it closely. It was thick, red, and rather greasy. Taking an envelope from the writing desk, he placed the hair inside and slipped the envelope into his pocket.

"We'll save that for the police," he said, picking up the phone.

While Frank was calling, Joe examined the hat further. From inside the band he pulled out a folded newspaper clipping.

When his brother hung up, Joe said, "Look at this, Frank!" He showed the clipping, headlined KIDNAPPER TRAPPED BY VOICEPRINT. "It tells how a guy was arrested on account of a spectrogram," Joe went on. "He kidnapped a young boy and telephoned the father for ransom. His voice was taped by the police and later the boy was found unharmed!"

Frank put the clue in his pocket next to the envelope. "The police will want this, too," he commented.

Two officers arrived in a squad car five minutes later. When the boys explained what had happened, one of them put out an all-points bulletin for the truck. Then they drove the police car behind the Voiceprint Lab and illuminated the scene with their spotlight.

Along with the boys, they searched for further clues. The rear door had been jimmied, but the burglars had left no other marks.

"A robbery squad officer will be over shortly," one of the policemen told Frank. "He'll make the investigation inside."

Soon a tall, leathery detective, who introduced himself as Lieutenant Howell, arrived at the scene. Frank and Joe described their encounter with the thieves, then accompanied him to their room, where they gave him the hat, the news clipping, and the strand of hair.

"I've called the lab manager," Lieutenant Howell said. "He'll be right over. We'll go and check the building with him."

They went back to the lab and met the manager at the door. He thanked the boys for their alertness and led them through the building. The alarm system had been cleverly disconnected, but nothing aside from the spectrograph had been disturbed.

One of the policemen came in to report that a bulletin had just come over the radio about the truck. "It was reported stolen earlier in the evening," he said, "and has just been found abandoned at the airport."

"Well, that's that," the lieutenant said gloomily. "If it hadn't been too dark for you boys to see the faces of those men, we could have all flights checked for persons answering their descriptions."

He told the lab manager he would arrange for a police guard until morning, since the rear door lock was broken, then left.

During the following week Lieutenant Howell had no news for the boys on the would-be thieves. Frank and Joe finished their course and received certificates attesting to the fact that they were qualified voiceprint operators.

The boys' plane landed at the Bayport airport at noon on Saturday. Chet Morton picked them up in his jalopy. It backfired as usual, sounding like a gang war in progress. When he pulled into the Hardy driveway, the uproar brought Aunt Gertrude to the front door.

Fenton Hardy's unmarried sister, who lived with the family, was tall and lean and had a heart as soft as a marshmallow under her decisive demeanor. She was also the best cook in Bayport, and that made her one of Chet's favorite people.

Aunt Gertrude showed how glad she was to see the boys back safely by making a flurry of dire predictions.

"Well," she declared as they carried their suitcases into the house, "you survived another trip in Chet's mechanical monster, I see. You'll all blow up in it yet, if you don't get yourselves stabbed at that fencing school first. Or killed by robbers like those in Somerville."

"How'd you hear about that, Aunt Gertrude?" Frank asked.

"The Somerville police phoned your father. He and your mother got away on their vacation, incidentally, so there will be only the three of us for lunch. Unless you've invited guests."

She looked pointedly at Chet, who sniffed the aroma of freshly made chili coming from the kitchen. He grinned. "I'm available if you're looking for somebody to invite."

"Then wash up and hurry," Aunt Gertrude commanded. "Lunch is in ten minutes."

Shortly before three that afternoon Frank and Joe were on their way to the Russo School of Fencing.

"You know," Frank said, "I've been thinking about the maestro's problem. I wonder if we couldn't give him a hand in finding the missing piece of that saber."

Joe grinned. "You just want to have a little vacation on the West Coast!"

"Well, if he has any idea at all of the area where the saber was broken, it might be a good idea!"

They parked the car and went inside. Biff, Tony, and Phil came in a few moments later.

Russo beckoned to the Hardys while the others were changing to fencing suits. "I'll have to leave tomorrow for Switzerland," he announced. "Are you boys still willing to keep the school open for me?"

"Mr. Russo," Frank began, "I'm sure the others can handle that. How would you like my brother and me to find the Adalante?"

"How do you expect to do that?"

"We thought if you had any clue at all—"

Russo shook his head. "I just don't know. All I can tell you is there's an old recluse named Miguel Jimenez who lives in the delta region of northern California. He is supposed to know the details of my grandfather's duel and also where the tip end of the broken sword was found."

"Haven't you asked him about it?" Frank put in.

"He refuses to talk to me," the fencing master said. "I don't know why." He scratched his head and looked thoughtfully at the boys.

"If I paid your fare to California, perhaps you could get the old man to tell you!"

"What's his address?" Joe inquired.

"I don't know. I only met him once in Stockton. He lives near there on a houseboat."

After some discussion, the Hardys decided to leave for California on Monday.

"You'll find that my grandfather was well known in that area," Russo said. "There's a book in the Stockton Public Library about him. His name was Giovanni Russo, and he was one of the richest men in the delta at the time he died. He made his fortune from the extensive vineyard he owned there."

"Okay, maestro," Joe said with a grin. "You just hired yourself a couple of detectives."

Russo smiled. "Good luck," he said. "And now you'd better change. This will be your last lesson before I leave."

That evening Chet stayed for dinner at the Hardy home. Aunt Gertrude had baked rhubarb pie, which was his favorite, and he ate three pieces. Miss Hardy pretended to be worried that he would burst, but secretly she was pleased that he liked the pie so much.

When the boys told her they were flying to California on Monday, her concern was not feigned. She imagined all kinds of dire things that could happen to them, including getting caught in an earthquake.

Fortunately Bayport's Chief of Police Ezra Collig stopped by after dinner and allayed her fears. The husky, keen-eyed friend of the family told her that he did not believe the doomsday prophets who kept predicting that California would slide into the ocean. "They're the same ones who always predict the end of the world." He chuckled. "And neither event is likely to happen in the near future."

Collig assured Miss Hardy that the boys were well able to take care of themselves.

He had come by to see the sound spectrograph. The boys took him and Chet to the lab to demonstrate it. After recording all their voices on tape, they made spectrograms of them.

"So that's my voice!" Chet said in amazement. "Look at those funny shapes."

"Your voice isn't the only thing about you that has a funny shape," Joe needled.

"Lay off," Chet grumbled. "I'm still growing, that's all."

On Monday morning Frank and Joe were packing when the phone rang.

"Maybe it's Dad," Frank said hopefully. They had tried to reach their parents to tell them about their trip, but with no success.

Frank scooped up the phone. It was Chief Collig.

"Bad news," Collig said curtly. "The Bayport Bank and Trust Company was just robbed. They got three hundred thousand dollars in cash, plus the box your father had in the storage room!"

CHAPTER IV

A Phony Voice

FRANK and Joe rushed downtown to meet the chief at the bank. They found the place in an uproar. Everyone was talking at once, trying to tell what happened.

Holding up both hands for silence, Collig said, "Take it easy. First I want to hear Mr. Dollinger's story."

Plump Henry Dollinger was the bank's vice-president. He said, "There were four bandits, all with nylon stockings over their heads. How they got in I don't know, but they were concealed in various places inside the bank when we got to work."

"When was that?" Collig asked.

"At eight-thirty. The bank doesn't open until nine, but employees get here a half-hour early to prepare for business. One of the gang was hiding in my office closet. I was dictating a letter into my dictaphone about a quarter of nine when he stepped out, put a gun to my head, and said, 'This is a stick-up. Make a wrong move and you've had it!' "

Dollinger mopped his forehead and went on. "He made me open the vault. I'm sure he must have known the time lock was set so it could be opened at a quarter of nine."

"Where were the rest of the bandits hiding?" the chief asked.

"I don't know. When we came out of my office, they were covering the other employees with guns and making them lie face down on the floor."

A woman teller said they had been hiding in the bank president's office.

A squat, muscular man who spoke with an accent said, "That was a good place for them to hide. The president is on vacation."

Chief Collig peered at him. "Who are you?"

Mr. Dollinger answered. "He is Signor Zonko, from the Ticino Bank in Bellinzona, Switzerland. He's here on an exchange program to study United States banking methods."

While the Swiss and the chief were shaking hands, Joe whispered to Frank, "His accent sounds Italian to me!"

"He's from the Italian section of Switzerland," Frank whispered back. "That's where Mr. Russo is going. Ticino is Italian for Tessin."

Chief Collig asked Zonko what he knew about the bank robbery, but the man said he had arrived after it was all over, a few minutes past nine.

The chief turned his attention back to the bank's vice-president. When he asked for descriptions of the bandits, Mr. Dollinger said the man hiding in his closet had been heavy-set, about five feet eight, and a hundred and eighty pounds. He had not particularly noticed the other three men.

The woman teller spoke up again. "One of them was tall, wide-shouldered, and had narrow hips. I noticed a wisp of red hair where the stocking was tied together over his head. It looked kind of greasy."

Joe blurted out, "Our eavesdropper in Somerville!"

"Your what?" Chief Collig looked blank.

Joe quickly explained about the man who had been sitting behind the partition in the motel restaurant and how later that night they had found a hat left at the spectrograph burglary scene.

"A strand of hair Frank found in the hat was red and greasy," Joe concluded. "We turned it over to the Somerville police."

Chief Collig agreed that it could be the same man. Then bank employees described the other two bandits. One was tall and thin, the other a heavy-set, burly man. Frank and Joe said the description fitted the two strangers who had pumped them about the Voiceprint Identification Course. When they described the men, the chief sent an officer to put all four descriptions on the air.

Frank now voiced a question that was uppermost in his mind. "What happened to the alarm system?" he asked.

"It was put out of commission," the chief replied. "Telephone lines were cut, too."

"I had to send one of my people out to call the police from a pay phone," Mr. Dollinger told them.

"Therefore," Chief Collig went on, "the thieves had been gone from the scene a full ten minutes before we even heard about it. And apparently no one saw the car they escaped in."

Frank turned to the bank's vice-president. "Mr. Dollinger, tell us about my father's records."

"The box was in our storage room in the basement," the man began. "Things like that are not kept in the vault. The basement is protected by iron bars and locked, of course."

A detective came over to report that there was no sign of forced entry.

"Looks as if they had inside help," the chief said. "Knowing how to put the burglar alarm out of commission and knowing when the lock on the vault was to be opened makes it almost certain. I'll want a complete rundown on all your employees, Mr. Dollinger."

Joe said, "Why don't we tape their voices and make voiceprints, Chief?"

"What for, Joe?" Frank asked. "We couldn't compare them with anything because Dad's catalog is gone!"

"Well, maybe we'll get it back," Joe said.

Chief Collig said, "It won't hurt. We'll also fingerprint everyone and have their prints checked by the FBI in Washington. Do you have your tape recorder with you?"

"No, sir," Joe said, "but we can rush home and get it while you're taking the fingerprints."

En route to the house, the boys discussed whether or not to get in touch with their father.

"I'd hate to spoil his vacation," Frank said. "Besides, what can he do?"

"You're right," Joe agreed.

They also decided to postpone their trip to the Coast until they found out the results of the police dragnet for the bank robbers. While Joe was getting the tape recorder, Frank called the airport and canceled their flight reservations.

When the boys got back to the bank, the police had finished fingerprinting all employees. Frank and Joe asked everyone to speak into the microphone of the tape recorder, saying the words: *it, me, you, the, on, I, is, and, a,* and *to*. These were the ten standard sounds used in making voiceprints.

When they had finished taping the last voice,

Frank suddenly had an idea. He turned to the bank's vice-president. "Mr. Dollinger, didn't you say you were using your dictaphone when the bandit stepped from your office closet?"

"That's right."

"Was the dictaphone still on when he spoke to you?"

Mr. Dollinger said thoughtfully, "I see what you're getting at. Yes, it was. I switched it off before I got up from my desk, but it was on when he told me it was a stick-up."

"Then his voice would be recorded!"

"Come on, let's see!" Dollinger said eagerly and led the boys and Chief Collig into his private office. He set the dictaphone on playback.

After the last two sentences of the letter a guttural, obviously disguised voice broke in. "This is a stick-up. Make the wrong move and you've had it!' "

"Great!" Joe exclaimed.

Frank asked Dollinger to run it once more so they could record it.

"That's just fine," he said when he was finished. "If the stick-up man is one of your employees, we'll find out soon!"

When Frank and Joe got home, it was lunchtime. They took a sandwich to their lab and made spectrograms of all the employees on the tape, including the one on the dictaphone.

The latter matched the voiceprint of the visiting Swiss, Signor Zonko! Obviously the man's Italian accent had been assumed, because the voice on the dictaphone was American.

"How do you like that for nerve?" Frank said in amazement. "He helped rob the bank, then took off his mask and walked right back in. No doubt he was the heavy-set member of the gang that Dollinger described."

Frank phoned Collig to report their discovery. The chief thanked him and said he would call back as soon as Signor Zonko was under arrest.

The phone rang an hour later. Frank answered.

"Zonko didn't return to the bank after lunch," Chief Collig reported. "We raided his apartment, but it was empty and all his belongings gone!"

"Oh brother!" Frank said. "As soon as we mentioned voiceprints, he must have known the jig was up."

"Right. And here's another piece of news. I telephoned the president of the Ticino Bank in Bellinzona. They were closed, because it's nine o'clock at night there now, but the operator got him at home. There's a bank officer there named Zonko, but he never left Switzerland. Our Zonko's credentials were faked."

"Looks as if we're dealing with international criminals," Frank said. "Since the only real evidence we have against them is the fake Zonko's voiceprint, I think we'll put it and the other spectrograms in Dad's safe-deposit box at the bank."

"Good idea," Collig replied. "You'd better hide that sound spectrograph somewhere, too. After failing to steal one in Somerville, the gang may try for yours!"

"I hadn't thought of that," Frank said. "Thanks for the suggestion."

When Frank hung up, he and Joe carried the spectrograph into the master bedroom and hid it behind a secret panel in their father's closet. Then they drove down to the bank and put the tape and voiceprints they had made that day into Fenton Hardy's safe-deposit box.

Next morning, after breakfast, the boys went to the lab to get some notes they had left there. When Joe opened the door, he stopped dead in his tracks and gaped.

The place had been torn apart. Every cabinet door stood open, the locks broken, and papers were strewn all about!

CHAPTER V

Gang War

"GOOD night!" Frank exclaimed. "And we never heard a thing!"

Joe shook his head. "I'm glad we didn't leave that tape and the voiceprints here."

"The spectrograph, too," Frank added. "Whoever did this obviously never thought of looking in the house for it."

"Well, let's clean up the mess," Joe said. "And then we'd better check on a flight to California!"

When the boys finished putting the laboratory back in order, Frank phoned Chief Collig, who had no news, then called the airport and made reservations for the ten-o'clock flight the next morning. He had just hung up when a well-dressed young man looked in the door.

"Hi, Scoop," Frank said. "Come on in."

Cub reporter Scoop Scales of the *Bayport*

Times entered the living room. "My editor sent me over to do a feature story on you guys," he said.

"On us?" Joe said in surprise. "What for?"

"You're too modest," Scoop replied with a smile. "The way you two identified that fake Swiss at the Bayport Bank and Trust Company as one of the robbers deserves a special story."

"Look, Scoop," Frank began, "we're not too keen on any publicity. We don't want the whole world to know what we're doing!"

"Don't worry, I'll keep it general enough. No trade secrets. Just the regular stuff, you know. Whether you like baseball and chocolate shakes, et cetera."

Frank sighed. "All right. Go ahead if you must."

The boys answered questions about their recent activities, including their attendance at the Voiceprint Lab, but said nothing about their impending trip. Scoop told them he would like to have a newspaper photographer take a picture of the Hardys' house the next day.

"Aunt Gertrude will be here," Frank said. "Just contact her."

The following morning Callie Shaw came by in her car to drive the boys to the airport. Slender, blond Callie was Frank's steady date. With her was Iola Morton, Chet's dark-haired sister, whom

Joe regarded as his best girl. Chet did not come along because he was on duty at the fencing school.

When it was time to say good-by at the loading gate, Callie said, "You boys stay out of trouble, hear!"

"You know they never do that," Iola remarked with a laugh. She turned to the Hardys. "Just get out of any trouble you get into!"

As the plane passed over Denver, Joe was commenting on the amazing speed of jet travel compared to the covered wagons of a hundred years ago.

Suddenly Frank interrupted him. "I just thought of a possible motive for the bank robbers going after those tapes and voiceprints!" he said excitedly.

"What?"

"Wouldn't the criminals whose voices are recorded gladly pay to have the tapes and their spectrograms destroyed?"

After thinking it over, Joe said, "The old shakedown racket, you mean?"

"Exactly. The gang could make big-shot crooks all over the country pay through the nose for those parts of Dad's catalog that apply to them!"

"You may have hit it," Joe agreed.

When they landed at San Francisco they were paged over the public-address system. "Frank and

Joe Hardy please come to the United Air Lines counter," a pleasant voice said.

While the announcement was being repeated, the boys were already entering the terminal. At the reservation desk they found a message to call Aunt Gertrude immediately.

"That's strange," Joe commented. "I wonder what's so urgent."

"Let's find out," Frank replied, pointing to a telephone booth. The boys squeezed in and Frank called home.

Aunt Gertrude sounded panicky. "Come back immediately!" she demanded. "Someone's going to blow up our house!" She spoke so loud that Joe could hear her too.

"What?" Frank asked incredulously. "Who's going to blow up the house?"

"I don't know. A man called a little while ago. What should I do, Frank?"

"Did you call Chief Collig?"

"N-no. Didn't think of it. All I could think of was getting in touch with you!"

"All right. Call him immediately. We'll be at the Occidental Hotel. Phone us there. There's nothing we can do for you from here, but the chief can give you police protection. Okay?"

"Yes," Aunt Gertrude said weakly. "I'll do it right away."

Frank hung up. "Trouble," he muttered glumly.

"Who's going to blow up the house?"
Frank asked

Joe nodded. "Let's get to the hotel and wait for her call."

While the boys were getting settled in their room at the Occidental, Joe had an idea. "I'll call Chet," he said. "Maybe he can run over to our house and see what's going on."

Chet answered the phone. When Joe explained the situation to him, he promised to check on Aunt Gertrude right away.

A half-hour later Chet called back. Joe held the receiver so Frank could listen in.

Chet was laughing so hard he could hardly get out what he wanted to say. Between guffaws he wheezed, "Aunt Gertrude—the paper—she misunderstood—"

Joe said to Frank, "I take it she isn't in any danger." Then he spoke into the mouthpiece. "This is probably costing you about a dollar a minute, Chet!"

This instantly sobered their pal. "It was Scoop Scales," Chet said. "He phoned your aunt because he wanted to take a picture of your house for the feature he's writing. When he said he was going to shoot the place and blow it up, she panicked and hung up on him. He meant blow up the negative into an enlargement!"

Relieved that Aunt Gertrude was not in any danger, Frank and Joe could not help laughing, too.

"Thanks, Chet." Joe chuckled.

"That's only one of the things I called about," Chet went on. "My father says he'll pay my fare out there if you need me."

"Why should we need you?" Joe asked.

"Aw, come on," Chet said. "I have him all talked into it. Tony, Phil, and Biff will handle the fencing school without me. You need my help, don't you?"

"All right," Joe said, relenting. "I guess we could use you."

"I'll be in tomorrow on the same flight you took. Meet me at the airport."

"We'll be there," Joe told him.

Since they would have to drive to Stockton, which was eighty-three miles from San Francisco via the freeway, the boys decided to rent a car. They got a new Ford sedan and drove to police headquarters to check in as visiting detectives.

When the officer on duty at the information desk learned they were the sons of the famous Fenton Hardy, he took them to see Chief of Detectives Henry Copeland.

Copeland was a muscular, ruddy-faced man. He greeted the boys cordially and inquired about their father, whom he knew well. Frank told him Mr. Hardy was in fine health and was presently on vacation at the Grand Canyon. Then he explained their reason for being in California.

"You may have trouble locating this Miguel Jimenez if he lives on a houseboat," Copeland said thoughtfully. "Do you know anything about the delta region?"

Both boys shook their heads.

"It's a triangular area of about five hundred square miles between Stockton, Sacramento, and Antioch. Once it was all under water, but many years ago it was partially drained, leaving hundreds of small islands surrounded by about a thousand miles of waterways."

"Good grief!" Joe said. "We'll never find him."

"The thing is," Copeland went on, "if he's a recluse, he might not be listed at the Stockton Post Office."

Frank looked glum. "It would take us a year to search all the waterways."

"Try the mailman," Copeland suggested.

During the conversation the boys mentioned that they had recently attended the Voiceprint Laboratories school in New Jersey. Copeland was greatly interested, since the San Francisco Police Department had just acquired a sound spectrograph.

They discussed voiceprint technology for a while, then Frank and Joe thanked the detective for his advice and left.

When Chet Morton arrived by jet the next afternoon, he brought with him a cablegram addressed to the Hardy boys from Bellinzona, Switzerland. It read:

OLD BOOK IN LIBRARY HERE HAS PHOTO TIP END OF ADALANTE WITH ADAL ON IT. GUARD END SHOULD HAVE ANTE. HAVE NOT LET COUSIN KNOW I AM HERE BECAUSE FEAR FOUL PLAY. CABLE ME HOTEL ANGELO IF YOU FIND GUARD.

ETTORE RUSSO

"Any news, so far?" Chet asked his friends.

"None, except that we might have trouble locating our man."

"Well," Chet said breezily, "you didn't expect this job to be easy, did you?"

When they got back to the Occidental Hotel, a uniformed policeman was waiting for the Hardys in the lobby. He said he had been sent by Chief of Detectives Henry Copeland.

"What's up?" Joe asked.

"Our voiceprint identification expert is in the hospital with a broken leg," the officer said. "The boss wants you to look at the spectrogram of a suspected extortionist."

He drove the three boys to headquarters in a squad car. The Hardys introduced Chet to the detective chief, then were led to the crime lab. It took Frank and Joe only a few minutes to decide that the voice of the extortionist was not that of the suspect who had been arrested.

"Well, that leaves the case still open," Copeland said ruefully. "But I'm glad to be able to free an innocent man. Thanks for your help, fellows."

The Hardys were about to leave when a call came over the "hotshot" speaker, saying: "Attention all units in vicinity of Chinatown. Gun battle between rival gangs reported across from Fat Ching's Chinese Theater."

"Gang war!" the chief exclaimed. "I'd better get over there."

"May we come along?" Frank asked eagerly.

Copeland hesitated, then said, "All right, but let's get rolling!"

He and another officer jumped into a squad car. The three boys squeezed into the back and they were on their way, with siren squealing.

Soon they reached the northeast corner of the city, where San Francisco's famous Chinatown was located. Its narrow streets were crowded with restaurants, theaters, temples, and small shops selling everything from herbs to dried fish.

"There's Fat Ching's Chinese Theater," Copeland said, pointing, as they turned into a narrow street.

At that moment a machine gun began to fire from a nearby building. Bullets blew out both front tires of the squad car!

CHAPTER VI

A Pretty Welcome

THE car slewed out of control, skidded sideways through the street for about fifty yards, and halted with a jolt when its left rear side slammed into a lamppost.

Both doors on that side popped open. All five passengers dived through them and crouched behind the car for protection.

Copeland and the policeman driver drew their guns.

The building from which the shots had come was a warehouse which looked deserted, directly across the street from Fat Ching's Chinese Theater. Four figures ran from the warehouse.

They were too far away for the boys to make out their faces. All wore hats. One was tall and thin, one squat and muscular, the third was heavyset and burly, and the fourth had broad shoulders and narrow hips. The latter two carried Thompson submachine guns.

The tall, thin man and the squat man jumped into the front seat of a black sedan parked in front of the abandoned warehouse. The burly fellow sprayed the Chinese theater across the street with another round of fire. The broad-shouldered man threw a burst of shots at the wrecked police car.

The boys and the two officers flattened themselves against the pavement as bullets ripped into the vehicle from one end to the other. Then there was the roar of a motor. Cautiously getting to their knees to peer over the hood and around both ends of the car, they saw the black sedan speeding away.

On his feet now, Detective Copeland said, "Let's see who they were shooting at in the theater."

Gun thrust out before him, he led the way toward the building. The driver followed, his pistol ready, too. The Hardys and Chet brought up the rear.

Squad cars with sirens screaming roared to a halt from both directions as they reached the theater. Officers armed with riot guns spilled from them. Copeland ordered the team from one car to check the warehouse and to send out an alert for the black sedan. Then he sent the other team around back of the theater to cut off the escape of anyone who might still be inside.

Ordering Frank, Joe, and Chet to stay outside, the chief and his driver went into the theater. Moments later the driver came out and motioned the boys to come in.

In the lobby Copeland was bending over the figure of a small, ferret-faced man. He was bleeding from a bullet wound in his chest.

Looking up, the chief said, "Ziggy Felton, a member of the Rocky Morgan gang. He says three of his buddies were with him, but they ran out the back way." Glancing at the driver, Copeland said, "Go call an ambulance."

As the policeman moved away, Copeland turned back to Felton. "What was it all about, Ziggy?"

In a weak voice the little man replied, "It's a new mob from the East Coast. They've got a tape of Rocky's voice and also his voiceprint. They wanted fifty grand, or else they were going to turn both over to the cops."

Ziggy wheezed. "We got the word they were holed up in that warehouse across the street, and Rocky decided to hit them instead of paying off. They were too tough, though. Drove us in here, then they got me '

Joe said to Frank, "Did anything seem familiar about those four men?"

Frank nodded. "Same sizes and shapes as our Bayport bank robbers. The thin man who drove the getaway car and the burly machine gunner could have been the pair who quizzed us in the restaurant in Somerville. The other machine gunner could have been the guy with the red, greasy hair. And the squat one looked like Signor Zonko!"

Under further questioning Ziggy Felton denied knowing the identities of any of the East Coast mob. However, he admitted having heard via the underworld grapevine that gangleaders in Chicago and New Orleans had also been shaken down.

By the time the ambulance arrived, the police, who had checked the warehouse, reported no one was there now. The theater building also was empty.

Copeland had one of the squad cars at the scene take him and his driver back to headquarters. En route the Hardys and Chet were dropped off at their hotel.

The following morning the three boys drove to Stockton in the rented Ford. The post office had no record of a Miguel Jimenez, but they were told by a clerk that mailman Herbert Shay would probably know him.

On a map the clerk showed them Shay's sixty-five-mile route and pointed out a waterway. "In about an hour you should catch up with him around here," he said. "There's a marina where you can rent a boat."

The boys thanked him and a short time later

were chugging along in a twelve-foot skiff at barely fifteen miles an hour.

Frank sat in the stern, running the fifteen-horsepower engine, Joe sat in the bow, and Chet was amidship.

"I'd prefer the *Sleuth,*" said Chet, referring to the Hardys' fast, sleek motorboat.

Joe nodded. "Especially since someone's been following us ever since we left the marina," he said apprehensively.

The others glanced back at an eighteen-foot inboard boat about a quarter mile behind them. It was idling along at a speed no greater than theirs. Through the windshield they could see only one person, but they were too far away to make out his features.

The boys' skiff had chugged to about the center of the lakelike area, a good three hundred yards from shore, when the speedboat suddenly roared with power and came leaping after them.

Traveling at about forty miles an hour it took their pursuer less than a minute to close the quarter-mile gap. It shot past on their left only twenty feet away, then swung across their bow so close it barely missed ramming them.

The pilot was hunched low and had a peaked white yachting cap pulled down to hide his face. As he swung in front of them the yachting cap blew off, and they had a brief glimpse of red hair.

A wave caused by the speeding boat hit them

simultaneously from the left side and the front. Frank made a valiant attempt to head the bow into it, but the skiff handled too sluggishly. The boat rode up the wave sideways to its crest and overturned.

The boys struggled to the surface a few yards apart just as the capsized boat sank from sight. They treaded water for a while until the waves subsided. The speedboat was rapidly disappearing in the distance.

When it was out of sight, and the water had calmed, Chet sputtered, "Now what?"

"We swim for shore," Frank said. "But first let's take some sightings so we can find this spot again."

Looking east toward a large island, he saw a flagpole before a row of small cottages. Glancing west, he noticed that the south edge of a boat dock on a smaller island exactly lined up with the flagpole. Then he looked north and south and fixed his position by means of trees on islands in both directions.

"Okay," he called. "Let's head for that larger island."

Weighted down by clothing, it was a long swim. Finally they waded ashore and walked across the sandy beach.

Suddenly Chet, who was in the lead, stopped dead in his tracks. Behind a sandy dune, stretched out on a blanket, were three girls in swimsuits.

They looked up in surprise, and the brunette on the left said, "Look who's here. Neptune and two of his mermen!"

"Wow!" Chet said, a grin spreading over his face. "We sure came to the right place!"

The plump blonde in the middle laughed. "I doubt it. This is a girls' camp." She added impishly, "Boys aren't allowed."

"Sorry about that," Joe said. "We're shipwrecked."

The slender redhead on the right gave Chet a searching look through long lashes.

"I'm Chet Neptune—I mean Morton," Chet introduced himself. "These two mermen are Frank and Joe Hardy. We're from Bayport back East."

"Hi, there," said the blond girl, whose name was Susie Wade. The redhead introduced herself as June Fall, and the brunette was Kay Dover.

"You look pretty sad," Kay decided, eying the boys' dripping clothes. "Come on. The Murrays might help you out."

"Who are they?" Frank asked.

"The camp owners."

The girls led the way to a large building surrounded by small cottages.

"Look what we found," June said to the tall, friendly woman inside.

Mrs. Murray shook her head in mock horror. "You find boys everywhere!" she said with a chuckle. Then she produced three pairs of swim trunks for the visitors to wear while she dried their clothing. Mr. Murray loaned them a canoe, a coil of stout rope, and a pair of pliers.

"This might help you get your boat ashore," he said.

Frank grinned. "Thanks. We sure appreciate it."

Frank sat in the stern of the canoe with one of the paddles, Joe scrambled amidship with the other, and Chet sat down in front. When they neared the point where the boat had sunk, Frank asked Joe to let him handle the canoe alone. He went back and forth, checking his landmarks, until all four lined up exactly.

Shipping his paddle, he said, "Okay, this is it."

Chet rose to a crouch and dived over the bow. It was about half a minute before he came up again.

"We're right on top of it," he sputtered. "Give me the pliers and the end of the rope."

Joe handed him both. Chet dived again. This time he was down for a full minute. A moment after he came up, the boat, minus its motor, rose to the surface upside down. Gasping for air, Chet dropped the pliers into the canoe and hung on to its side.

Joe pulled on the rope from the other side and hauled the outboard motor up. They righted the boat and attached the motor and towed the disabled craft ashore.

"Good work, Chet," Frank praised.

"Admit it, you'd be lost without me!" Chet began to sing. "Back to paradise . . ."

"Listen, Don Juan, we're here on a job," Joe reminded him.

"Who says you can't combine work with pleasure?" Chet replied loftily.

When they reached the beach, the boys received a very pleasurable surprise. The girls had prepared a delicious picnic lunch. There were plenty of sandwiches, and a good thing too, because Chet and the plump blonde ate four each. She kept urging more food on the husky boy, obviously having picked him as her particular companion.

"They're sure suited to each other," Joe whispered to Frank. "I'd hate to pay the grocery bill, though!"

Kay, overhearing the whispered remark, giggled.

Frank asked June if the mailman had been there yet. She told him that he stopped at the camp on his return trip and would be along about two in the afternoon.

The boys decided to wait for him there rather than trying to catch up with him on his route.

After lunch they drained the mixture of gasoline, oil, and water from the outboard's tank and cleaned the motor. Mr. Murray supplied them with fresh gas and oil.

By then their clothing was dry. When the mailman arrived, they were ready to leave. Herbert Shay was a well-built, middle-aged man. His boat was a sixteen-footer with a powerful seventy-five-horsepower outboard motor and front-seat controls.

He told the boys that old Miguel Jimenez's houseboat was moored in a secluded lagoon off Hank's Tract Lake, and described how to get there. The lake, he explained, had once been the site of numerous farms and orchards. But in 1936 the levees surrounding the area broke, flooding the tract so badly that attempts to redrain it had to be abandoned.

"The lake can get awfully rough," he warned. "And if fog comes up, you can get lost without a compass. Do you have one?"

When the boys confessed they did not, he suggested that if there was any sign of fog when they reached the lake, they should stay near the shore instead of crossing directly to the lagoon.

Then the mailman moved on. The Bayporters thanked the girls and the Murrays for their hospitality and resumed their journey. They reached Hank's Tract Lake without incident, and, since the sun was shining, headed directly across to the shallow lagoon.

There was only one houseboat in sight, a rickety old contraption tied to a tree. They beached the motorboat and climbed out. A plank led from shore to the wobbly porch of the houseboat.

As they approached, a tiger-colored cat emerged from a nearby clump of tules, padded up the plank, and stood before a hole in the screen door. The feline paid not the slightest attention to the boys, but peered intently into the interior of the houseboat. Then it crept through the ripped screen and disappeared inside, its tail swishing.

"Probably the old man's cat," Chet mused. "I understand that all hermits have some kind of pet. They'd go nuts living absolutely alone. Take Robinson Crusoe for example. He—"

"Sh, sh!" Frank commanded.

"What's up?" Chet whispered, stopped short in his philosophical observation.

"I heard something."

"Like what?"

The three stood still and listened. From inside came a loud noise. This was followed by a shrill high-pitched voice. "Go away! Go away!"

The shriek sent shivers through the boys.

CHAPTER VII

Danger in the Delta

"IF that's old Jimenez, he sounds like a fiend," Chet whispered.

A cracked voice behind them said, "That's not old Jimenez, young man. It's Don Quixote."

The boys turned to face an elderly but straight-backed man with snow-white hair. His deep-set eyes burned at them.

"You heard Don Quixote," he said. "Get going!"

"Are you Mr. Jimenez?" Frank asked.

"What's it to you, boy?"

"I'm Frank Hardy. This is my brother Joe, and Chet Morton. We're trying to get some information on Giovanni Russo, and his sword Adalante. We heard you know all about it."

The old man glared at him for a second before saying, "I have no information. Go away."

"Help! Help!" the shrill voice shrieked from inside.

"Por dios!" Jimenez exclaimed. "Don Quixote!"

He started up the plank, but moved so stiffly that it was obvious he would not arrive in time to save Don Quixote from whatever danger he was in. Frank leaped past him, jerked open the screen door, and rushed inside.

A large black myna bird was perched on a bookcase, flapping his wings and screeching in terror. The tiger-colored cat crouched on a table, ready to spring.

Frank's outstretched arm blocked the cat's leap. It dropped to the floor, hissing, then fled between the legs of Miguel Jimenez as the old man pulled open the door.

"You saved Don Quixote," he said gratefully. "Thank the young man, Don Quixote!"

The bird ruffled his feathers and squawked, "Good-by and good riddance!" Then he cocked his head at Frank and said, "Welcome aboard, mate!"

"Thanks, Don Quixote," Frank replied with a grin.

Jimenez glanced over his shoulder at Joe and Chet, who had paused in the doorway. "Come on in," he invited them.

The rescue of his bird completely changed the recluse's attitude. When the Hardys offered to mend the hole in his screen door, he mellowed even more. He produced a piece of wire screening and they patched the hole. As they were working, he told them the true story of the so-called duel in which the sword Adalante had been broken and lost.

"There never was a duel," the old man began. "That's a story told to conceal what really happened. Giovanni Russo was kidnapped by a bandit and was held for ransom in a secret place in his own vineyard."

He paused, then continued thoughtfully. "Fearing death, Giovanni wrote his will on his saber. Or so he later said, anyway. The blade was broken when he fought his way free. Then he swam from the island on which his vineyard was located to another island."

"Where was his property?" Frank asked.

Jimenez explained that it was near a place called Paradise Point, and described how to get there.

As he finished, the myna bird suddenly flapped his wings and shrieked toward a window, "Go away! Go away!"

"Someone must be out there!" the old man declared. "Don Quixote never says that unless we have a visitor."

The boys rushed outside to investigate. But there was no sign of anyone around.

When they returned to the houseboat, Joe asked, "How do you know all about the kidnapping, Mr. Jimenez?"

In a sad voice the recluse replied, "To my shame the bandit who kidnapped Giovanni Russo was named Miguel Jimenez, too. He was my great-uncle."

"We heard there's a book about Russo in the Stockton Public Library," Chet put in. "Do you know about that, Mr. Jimenez?"

The old man nodded. "It's in the school library of the College of the Pacific in Stockton, not the public library. It has a description of the sword Adalante in it."

The recluse eyed the boys curiously. "Why are you so interested in all this?"

Frank quickly told him the reason. Jimenez shook his head doubtfully and said, "I can't imagine how you expect to find the saber. But good luck, anyway."

The boys thanked him for his information and left. When the skiff chugged out of the lagoon, Frank shifted the motor into neutral and glanced up at the sky. It had become quite overcast.

"Looks as if a storm's brewing," he said.

"The mailman only warned us against fog," Chet remarked. "Rain shouldn't stop us."

"I guess so," Frank agreed and headed away from shore.

As they neared the center of the lake, a speedboat emerged from a hidden cove near the mouth of the lagoon and arrowed straight for them.

"That's the one that swamped us before!" Chet exclaimed.

"There's another boat coming from the opposite direction!" Joe called.

Frank and Chet turned to look. A sixteen-footer with a powerful outboard motor was also heading toward them.

The speedboat reached them first. This time, even though he was crouched low, the boys could see the driver's face because he was hatless. It was a coarse, brutal face surmounted by red hair!

On the previous occasion Frank had not realized until too late that the man was deliberately trying to swamp them. But this time he was prepared. As the boat zoomed near, Frank cut sharply left to aim the bow at the point he judged the speedboat would swing in front of them.

There was a near collision. The speedboat curved no more than a foot from the skiff's bow. Then, as it swept past, the skiff nosed over the crest of the wave and plunged down its other side without capsizing.

But just as the water began to calm, the speedboat roared toward them again! By now the other boat had reached the spot, too. The boys recognized mailman Herbert Shay. Realizing what was happening, he came to their rescue. He headed for the approaching craft at full throttle.

Although smaller than the speedboat, Shay's seventy-five-horsepower outboard motor made his boat just as fast. And the mailman showed reckless courage. He bore head-on at the larger craft, forcing the redhead to spin his wheel in panic to the right.

Then Shay swung sharply left as the speedboat was turning. The two canted side by side, showing their bottoms to each other and almost touching before veering apart again.

The larger boat nearly capsized before its pilot managed to get it back under control. Unable to stomach the dangerous game, he opened his engine wide and roared away.

The mailman pulled alongside the Hardys. "Who was that idiot?" he asked.

"Don't know," Frank called out. "The same kook gave us some trouble on the way out to the Jimenez houseboat."

"It's getting to be a wacky world," Shay said, throttling down to keep his boat abreast of the boys' skiff. "Some people take pleasure in hurting others for no good reason."

Joe said, "I think there's a reason behind this."

"And we'll find out what it is, too!" Chet said emphatically.

"Take care," Shay said. "By the way, what luck did you have with Jimenez?"

"We saved his myna bird," Frank said with a grin. "There seems to be a shortage of cat food around here." He told what had happened.

The mailman grinned. "Your good deed for the

day!" Then he glanced up at the sky. "You'd better get across the lake fast. It's going to storm any minute."

With a good-by wave, he sped off. Frank headed the skiff for the far end of the lake.

A few seconds later there was a light patter of rain, accompanied by a distant rumbling sound. Then came a blinding flash of lightning and almost simultaneously an earsplitting crack of thunder!

CHAPTER VIII

A Library Clue

THE lightning bolt hit so close in front of them that they could smell the ozone. Frank instinctively steered around the spot.

This was a lucky move. The lightning's target had been a nearly submerged log, now split in two by the bolt. Both halves were large enough to drive a hole in the bottom of the skiff.

The trio reached the marina without further incident, turned in their boat, and drove back to Stockton. They checked into a motel on the outskirts of town.

Saturday morning, while breakfasting in the motel dining room, they discussed plans for the day. It was decided that Joe and Chet would check out the vineyard once owned by Giovanni Russo while Frank investigated the book old Miguel Jimenez had told them was in the library of the

College of the Pacific. Joe and Chet dropped Frank off at the campus, then drove on to Paradise Point.

The college was coeducational and had an enrollment of only about fifteen hundred students. It had a beautiful campus, with a mixture of ancient vine-covered buildings and recently constructed modern ones. The school was open because summer sessions were being held.

In the library Frank checked the card catalog. Under *Russo, Giovanni* he found listed a book titled *Master of the Vineyards* by an author named José Flores. It was in the basement stacks, in the rare-book section.

Frank went downstairs. At the end of an alcove formed by floor-to-ceiling shelves he spotted a girl seated at a reading desk. Her back was to him, but there was something familiar about her slim figure and red hair. He walked over for a closer look.

Hearing his footsteps, the girl looked up. It was June Fall from the girls' camp!

"What are you doing here?" Frank asked in surprise.

"I have a summer job as a research assistant for one of the professors," June replied with a smile. "He's doing a paper on early vineyards in the delta area. But what about you?"

"Oh, just looking for a book," Frank said vaguely. He glanced at the heavy, leather-bound volume open on the desk before the girl. "What's that?"

"It's called *Master of the Vineyards* and is about an Italian Swiss named Giovanni Russo, who was once the richest vineyard owner in the delta. Professor Von Stolk is particularly interested in him."

Was this just coincidence? Frank wondered. Or was the professor also on the trail of the sword Adalante?

Before he could ask any questions, a tall, thin, aesthetic-looking man with a distinguished head of gray hair appeared at the end of the alcove. He wore a sports coat and an elaborately knotted scarf around his throat.

"Oh hi, Professor," June said. "I think I've found something."

The man gave Frank a suspicious look, so the young detective said good-by and discreetly departed. He went into the next alcove and stood with his ear to the shelf. All he could hear was a low murmur of conversation.

Then the professor and the girl left. As soon as they disappeared up the stairs, Frank returned to the first alcove. The book still lay open on the reading desk.

The left page was 254. The right page was numbered 259! Frank realized four pages were missing!

Checking the index, he discovered that the

missing pages contained a description and a photograph of the sword Adalante, plus the story of how the sword had been lost.

Professor Von Stolk must be on the trail of the guard end of the sword, too, Frank thought. Was the girl an accomplice, or merely an unwitting tool? He decided the quickest way to find out was to ask her and hurried outside.

Frank roamed up and down the shaded walks of the campus looking for either the professor or the pretty redhead. Finally he spotted her walking along a few yards ahead of him.

He strode up behind her and called, "Hey, wait a minute!"

Halting, the girl turned around, smiled, and said, "Yes?"

She was just as pretty as June, but Frank had never seen her before in his life!

"Sorry," he stammered. "I thought you were someone else."

"I am someone else," the girl replied, still smiling. "I'm Holly Brewer."

Frank smiled back. "My name is Frank Hardy. Can you tell me where the administration building is?"

"I'll show you. I work there. I'm the faculty records clerk."

"Oh?" Frank said. "Then you are the one I'm looking for. Where will I find Professor Von Stolk?"

Holly looked puzzled. "We have no one by that name."

"Are you sure?"

"Positive. We have a hundred and twenty-three instructors, and I keep the records of all of them."

Frank described the man, but Holly could think of no one on the faculty that fitted the description. When Frank explained that he had seen the professor in the library, the girl suggested that perhaps he was from another college or university, and merely had been doing research here.

After thanking her, Frank decided to return to the motel. There was a bus stop across the street from the campus.

Frank stood at the curb waiting and idly watching traffic, when a motorcycle approached at high speed on his side of the street.

Just before it reached the corner, someone butted Frank hard in the back. He stumbled to hands and knees, directly into the path of the oncoming cycle!

It swerved in time, missing Frank by inches, and roared on across the intersection.

Leaping to his feet, the boy spun to see a broad-shouldered, thin-hipped man with red hair running down a side street. Frank raced after him.

The fleeing man leaped a fence and dashed across a yard. As Frank cleared the fence right behind him, out of the corner of his eye he saw a cruising police car pulling to the curb. Two officers got out to investigate what was going on.

The redhead vaulted another fence with Frank close at his heels. Halfway across the second yard the boy made a flying tackle and brought the man down with a crash.

He was sitting astride his assailant's back, twisting his arms behind him, when the two policemen approached. Each grasped one of Frank's arms and lifted him erect.

"What's going on?" the older officer inquired.

Then the redhead pushed himself to his knees and glanced over his shoulder. When the policemen saw his face, they released Frank and collared his prisoner.

"Red Bowes!" the younger officer exclaimed, pulling out a pair of handcuffs. He turned to Frank. "You caught yourself a prize. This guy's wanted for a half-dozen bank robberies."

"I'm not surprised," Frank said. "He's one of a gang that robbed the Bayport Bank and Trust Company. He tried to push me in front of a motorcycle just now!"

Frank explained who he was and why he was in California. Then he turned to Bowes. "You were listening outside the window when we talked to old Jimenez yesterday, weren't you?"

"What if I was?" the bank robber asked sullenly. "That's no crime."

"Why did you follow us?"

"That's for me to know and for you to find out," Red Bowes snarled.

The younger policeman said, "Who was with you on the Bayport job, Red?"

"None of your business!"

"And who was your buddy in Somerville when you tried to rob the Voiceprint Lab?" Frank put in.

"You can't tie me to that."

"The Somerville police can," Frank assured him. "You left your hat at the scene. A red hair was in it."

Bowes stared at the boy, fear in his eyes. Then he said defiantly, "I'm not the only guy with red hair." But Frank knew that Bowes realized his game was up.

The policemen asked Frank to come along to headquarters. Bowes was booked on a number of counts and informed of his legal rights.

"Yeah," he snarled. "I won't say a word without a lawyer!"

As an officer led him toward the cellblock, Bowes changed his mind, however. He sneered at Frank as he passed him. "How did you like the shape I left your lab in?" he asked.

"So it was you, was it?" Frank replied. "Was Zonko with you?"

Bowes walked on without answering.

Frank asked one of the policemen if he could use the telephone, and called the motel.

Joe answered. "Did you find a clue in the library?" he wanted to know.

"Yes. Also the guy who played games with us yesterday when we visited Jimenez," Frank replied, and told his brother what had happened.

"I've got news, too," Joe said when he had finished. "But it can wait until we get there. Chet and I'll pick you up."

"Is it good or bad news?" Frank inquired.

"Bad. You might even say terrible!"

CHAPTER IX

The Old Map

JOE was driving the Ford when he and Chet picked up Frank outside police headquarters.

As the car pulled away from the curb, Frank asked, "What's this bad news?"

"The vineyard's gone," Joe said. "Part is already a suburb, and the last of it is being used for a new housing development."

"As far as we could find out," Chet put in, "the only original building left is a wine storage cellar, and they're going to bulldoze it down this afternoon."

"That could be the secret place where Giovanni Russo was held prisoner by his kidnapper!" Frank exclaimed. "Did you ask to see it?"

"The foreman wasn't there," Joe said. "He was off trying to hire a bulldozer."

"Drive out there now," Frank said.

The island on which the Russo vineyard had

been was somewhat north of Paradise Point. Although it was in the delta area, it could be reached by car via a series of bridges. The boys arrived at the planned housing development about twelve-fifteen.

Streets had been laid out in the tract, although they were not yet paved. The unroofed raw wood skeletons of about two dozen houses were in various stages of construction. Work crews sat near them eating their lunches.

Joe parked in front of the contractor's office, a small prefabricated sheet-iron hut. A short distance away was an ancient one-story stone building.

"That must be the wine storage place over there," he said to Frank, pointing.

"Right. And next to it is a bulldozer!"

"Just in time," Joe said as they got out of the car and walked into the office.

Seated at a desk sipping coffee from a Thermos bottle was a lean, suntanned man. Another fellow had already finished his lunch. He was tall, blond and heavy-set and stood at the far end of the room, lunging with a fencing foil at a rope hanging from the ceiling.

The man at the desk glanced up as the boys entered, but the blond man continued to practice without paying any attention to them.

Frank asked, "Are you the foreman?"

The lean man nodded. "Jim Emory's my name."

"I'm Frank Hardy," the boy replied. He introduced Joe and Chet, then explained that they wanted permission to search the wine storage building before it was bulldozed down.

"Why?" Emory asked.

Frank told about their search for the broken blade.

"It's all right with me," the foreman said with a shrug. "We're only going to tear the place down, anyway."

The blond fellow stopped his practice and came over, still carrying the foil. In a surly voice he said, "You'd better be out of there by one o'clock. If you aren't you'll be buried under a heap of stones!"

"What's your hurry?" Joe asked, anger rising in him at the man's attitude.

"This is Harry Madsen, the bulldozer operator," Emory said soothingly, and gave the boys' names.

Madsen made no effort to acknowledge the introduction. Instead he said, "I have another job later this afternoon. So that building comes down at one o'clock whether you're out of it or not."

Looking at his watch, Frank said, "Let's get busy then, fellows. We only have a little over a half-hour."

On the first floor of the wine storage building there was nothing but some moldering, empty wine casks. They found a narrow stone stairway leading to the cellar. Joe went to the car and came back with a flashlight before they descended the stairs.

The cellar had vaulted ceilings and high, slitted windows which let in only dim light. Cobwebs hung everywhere. Most of the rooms were empty, but a couple contained rotting wooden racks and a few ancient, empty bottles.

The boys searched thoroughly. Finally Chet said, "Nothing here."

"There's one more room we haven't checked," Joe reminded him. They walked through a doorway and noticed a small wooden chest with rusty hinges just ahead of them.

"Let's have a look in there," Joe said, beaming his flashlight on the chest while Frank lifted the lid.

At first it appeared to be empty, but then they saw that the dirt in the bottom covered a single sheet of ancient brown parchment paper. Chet took the paper out and blew the dust off it. Then he held it for Joe to shine the light on.

"It's a map of the island!" Frank exclaimed.

"You're right. It shows Giovanni Russo's home, a barn, and some other structures," Joe said.

"This is the place we're in now," Chet remarked, pointing. "And there are two similar buildings, one on the northern part of the island, the other on the eastern edge."

"That means originally there were three wine storage cellars here," Frank declared. "I wonder if the other two are still in existence."

At that moment they heard a heavy engine starting outside. Joe turned the light on his watch.

"It's one o'clock," he said. "We'd better get out of here. Our pal means business!"

They heard the bulldozer back a few feet. The motor began to race, and suddenly exhaust fumes poured through one of the slitted windows.

Choking and coughing, the boys ran for the stairs. When they got outside, the bulldozer engine was still running, but Harry Madsen was out of the cab, standing next to it. He threw them a nasty grin.

"You did that on purpose!" Chet said angrily. "You deliberately backed up so exhaust fumes would go through that window!"

"So what, Fatty?" the blond man asked contemptuously. "Want to make something of it?"

Chet took a step toward him. Harry Madsen reached into the cab of the bulldozer and whipped out the foil he had been practicing with. He slashed it at Chet, who leaped back out of the way just in time to avoid getting it across the shoulders.

The foreman, who had come from the contractor's hut, said sharply, "That's enough, Harry!"

Ignoring him, Madsen looked from Frank to

Joe. "Either of you want trouble?" he challenged.

"Hand me a foil and I'll give you all the trouble you can handle," Joe said heatedly.

"You think so?" Madsen sneered. "I'll meet you any time you say."

"Right now!" Joe suggested.

"I only brought one foil with me. After I finish work I'll go home and get another one. Gloves and masks, too. Then I'll meet you here about four-thirty."

"That's fine with me," Joe told him.

Jim Emory was dubious. "You're letting yourself in for something, young fellow. Harry takes lessons!"

"So do I," Joe replied. "I'll be here at four-thirty, Madsen!"

When they left the housing development site, the boys drove to the east end of the island to see if they could locate the second wine storage building shown on the parchment map.

A number of homes had been erected in the area, but there was nothing resembling the storage place. The map had not been drawn to exact scale, so there was no way of telling precisely where it was located.

"No luck," Frank said after a while, disappointed.

"Let's try the other one," Joe suggested and drove to the north end of the island. This area

Exhaust fumes poured through the window

had not been built up because of its steep hills. But they could not find the exact site, and after driving up and down a few mountain roads, they gave up.

"Let's go somewhere for lunch," Chet said plaintively. "You realize it's after two o'clock?"

Joe grinned. "You just can't take all that sleuthing, Chet!"

They found a roadside restaurant and stopped for sandwiches.

When they had finished, Frank said, "Let's try the county clerk. There ought to be some kind of record of the buildings on the property when it was sold by old Giovanni."

Stockton was the county seat of San Joaquin County. They drove back into town and went to the courthouse. When they walked up the steps, Joe stopped suddenly.

"Frank—they'll be closed. It's Saturday."

"You're right. Well, since we're here, let's try anyway."

They were in luck. The county clerk was in to catch up on some work. He was a thin little man who wore glasses on the end of his nose. Frank showed him the parchment map and asked if there was a way to check if the other two wine storage buildings were still in existence.

"Sure," the clerk replied. "They would be on the original plats when the island owner deeded it over to whoever bought it from him. I'll start from there and go forward through subsequent property transfers."

He took the map and went into another room, while the boys settled into chairs. About ten minutes later he came back.

Handing the map back to Frank, he said, "They're still extant."

"Where?" Frank asked eagerly.

"Well, the one on the north part of the island is on a ski slope. It's now used as a hilltop station, and belongs to Carson's Lodge off Burns Mountain Road."

"What about the other one?" Joe asked.

"That's been converted into a private home."

"Who owns it?"

"I'm afraid I can't tell you without the owner's permission!"

CHAPTER X

A Treacherous Fence

FRANK said, "Aren't these public records?"

"Well, yes," the clerk admitted.

"Then anyone has access to them," Frank pointed out.

Reluctantly the clerk said, "The home is owned by a movie scenario writer named Vincent Steele. The reason I didn't want to tell you is that I happen to know him. He's an absolute nut about privacy. Please don't let on that I gave you this information. He might make trouble for me."

The boys assured him they would not tell Steele and the clerk gave them the address, which was 125 Port Street.

Shortly before four-thirty they returned to the construction site. There was no sign of the bulldozer, but Harry Madsen, Jim Emory, and a small, sinewy man stood next to a car. To the boys' surprise the wine storage building was still standing!

"How come this place hasn't been razed?" Frank asked.

"The contractor phoned," Emory answered. "He wants us to postpone the job till Monday."

"Why?"

"I don't know. Some archaeologist is supposed to come and talk to Harry at six o'clock."

Madsen was impatient. "You ready?" he asked.

"Any time you are," Joe said coldly.

Madsen had brought a set of foils, masks, and gloves. He pointed to the small man. "This is my friend Amos Cain. He'll direct the bout."

"What does he know about fencing?" Joe inquired.

"He happens to be the maestro of my school!" Madsen replied with a superior air.

Joe suggested that if Madsen was going to have a personal friend act as bout director, his brother and Chet should be judges. When Cain learned that both boys knew the rules, he agreed.

Then he marked an area six feet by forty feet in the dirt street to serve as the arena.

Joe and Madsen donned their wire-mesh masks and gloves and made some parries and counter-parries to get the feel of their blades.

By now the workday had ended. Instead of going home, the construction crew crowded around to watch the bout.

Madsen casually moved nearer to Joe as he began to make parries and thrusts and lunges. Then he swished the blade of his foil through the air.

Suddenly Chet shouted, "Look out, Joe!"

Joe leaped aside just in time to avoid a slash across the legs. Harry Madsen said mockingly, "Sorry, Hardy. Accident."

"That was no accident!" Chet said angrily, stepping toward the blond man.

Madsen swung the foil back over his shoulder with the evident intention of whipping Chet with it. Instead, Chet threw a rolling block into the man's knees. His feet were knocked out from under him. Madsen pitched forward over Chet, dropping his foil.

Both jumped to their feet and faced each other. Madsen swung a roundhouse right at Chet's head. The stocky boy ducked and punched Madsen in the stomach. Harry grunted and doubled over.

Frank pulled Chet away, but the blow had cooled Madsen's desire to bedevil Chet any more. He blustered and threatened but made no further attempt at violence.

"Forget it and pick up your foil," the foreman ordered.

Eventually the contestants were ready to begin fencing. Amos Cain took up the director's position.

Joe and his opponent both raised their foils vertically before their masks.

"Ready?" Cain asked.

The fencers got on guard, crossed their foils, and nodded Yes.

"Fence!" the director ordered.

The blades engaged, disengaged again. Madsen extended his arm and Joe parried. Then he engaged his opponent's blade in rapid order in what were called the fourth, sixth, and second positions and executed a filo and patinando with a disengage from the last position.

Madsen parried the blade but not before it struck his mask. The blond man stumbled backward, clutching at his mask with his left hand. Concerned that the tip of his foil might have penetrated and inflicted a face wound, Joe lowered his foil.

Instantly Madsen extended his arm and lunged.

"Halt!" Amos Cain ordered. "First touch against Hardy."

"Wait a minute!" Chet protested. "Madsen pretended to be hurt. Anyway, you should have halted the action as soon as Joe made that foul touch."

"You judges should have called the foul touch," the director pointed out. "Since you didn't, and I saw none, no halt was called. Harry's hit was perfectly legal."

"Legal, maybe," Chet muttered. "But not ethical."

"On guard!" the director ordered.

The foils crossed again. After several lunges and parries by both opponents, the blond man suddenly stepped back, lowered his foil, and began to remove his mask. Regarding him inquiringly, Joe lowered his foil too.

Madsen's blade instantly came up again, he stepped forward, thrust, and lunged.

"Halt!" the director ordered. "Point two for Harry. Two against Hardy."

Both Chet and Frank protested loudly.

"I hadn't called a halt," Amos Cain said reasonably. "Hardy shouldn't have dropped his guard."

"Let it go, fellows," Joe said grimly. "He won't catch me with any more sneaky tricks."

It was an accurate prediction. Several more times Madsen pretended to be hurt, but each time Joe kept his foil raised defensively when he disengaged. In rapid order Joe made five touches in a row.

Madsen objected to each one as off target, but by now the watching workmen realized what a poor sport Madsen was and booed him down every time.

After the fifth straight touch, Cain said reluctantly, "Bout. Hardy wins."

"On five fouls!" Harry yelled. "He cheated!"

"You're the cheater," Chet said. "The only two hits you made were by dirty play."

The blond man turned on Chet, his foil raised. Joe stepped forward, his raised also. But Madsen decided not to risk tangling with Joe again.

"I'll get even with you guys," he muttered as he turned away.

Joe tossed his foil and glove on the ground, dropped his mask next to it, and went over to get his coat from the workman who had been holding it for him.

"Come on. Let's get out of here," he said to Frank and Chet.

The boys said good-by to Emory and his men, then Joe slid behind the wheel of the Ford.

They drove in silence for a few moments. Then Frank said, "We should definitely go back there at six and see who the archaeologist is."

"You fellows can go," Chet said. "At six I plan to be eating."

"We can eat later," Joe told him.

"Not me," Chet declared. "I need something to keep up my strength after protecting you guys!"

Frank and Joe left Chet at a hamburger stand and returned to the construction site just before six. They parked a short distance away and crossed through a stand of trees edging the development. Halting near the housing area, they peered toward the contractor's office.

They were perhaps fifty yards from the sheet-metal shack. No one was around except Harry Madsen, who was leaning against the fender of his car in front of the office.

"Now why would this archaeologist talk to Harry instead of the foreman?" Joe asked in a low voice.

Frank shrugged. "The whole thing seems fishy to me," he said.

A sleek sports car drove up and a tall, thin, gray-haired man got out.

"Professor Von Stolk!" Frank murmured in surprise. "Now I'm sure his research in the library was not for an academic reason. That guy's after Russo's sword too!"

They watched as the professor showed two sheets of paper to Madsen.

"Maybe those are the pages torn from that book!" Frank speculated.

"Could be," Joe said. "Too bad we can't get closer to see."

Von Stolk and the bulldozer operator conversed for some time. Then the professor disappeared into the wine cellar. He emerged a few minutes later, handed Madsen something, and left. Harry followed in his own car.

Frank and Joe once more searched the cellar, but to no avail. "We may as well get Chet," Frank said.

It was six-thirty when they picked up their pal at the hamburger stand. Chet had consumed two cheeseburgers and a milk shake, and announced that he was now ready for dinner.

The boys found a restaurant and ate. During the meal Frank and Joe described the meeting they had observed between Harry Madsen and Professor Von Stolk. Chet shook his head in despair. "No doubt this professor is on the trail of our saber," he said. "But what possible motive could he have?"

"What are we going to do next?" Joe inquired.

"Yes," Chet put in. "Now that I've eaten, I'm ready for action again!"

"Let's look up this guy Steele," Frank suggested.

The boys paid their check and drove to 125 Port Street.

When they arrived, Chet said, "This place doesn't resemble the wine storage building, except for the ancient stone."

A second story with a peaked roof had been added, and there was a huge picture window in front. The house sat on about an acre of ground, surrounded by a split-rail fence. The driveway leading to a garage behind was blocked by an iron gate, and another iron gate barred the way to a walk leading to the front door.

Joe parked and they all got out. It was nearly eight o'clock, but still light. Drapes on the picture window in the living room were wide open. A woman seated on a couch was reading a magazine.

Joe tried the gate. It was locked.

Chet said, "The fence isn't very high. Let's climb it."

He put one hand on the top rail with the intention of swinging his legs over it. Instead he emitted a gasp and fell to the ground unconscious!

CHAPTER XI

Faked Out

FRANK pulled Chet away from the fence, while Joe stooped to look up under the top rail. A bare copper wire ran beneath it.

"It's electrified," Joe stated. "What a dirty trick!"

Frank had been holding an ear to the unconscious boy's chest. "His heart's still working all right," he said. "I guess the shock just knocked him out."

Rolling Chet over on his stomach, Frank began to give him artificial respiration.

The front door of the house opened and a middle-aged woman with graying hair came out. She walked to the gate, wringing her hands.

"I didn't know that was switched on," she said. "I'm terribly sorry. Is your friend hurt?"

Without stopping his rhythmic movements, Frank said, "You can see he's out cold. That fence is dangerous!"

"Oh dear!" the woman said. "I told my husband he was going too far with his desire for privacy. Are you going to sue us?"

"Depends on how our friend recovers," Frank replied.

Chet opened his eyes and said, "Hey, who's that sitting on my back?"

Frank rose to his feet. Chet rolled over and sat up.

"What happened?" he asked.

"The fence was charged with electricity," Joe told him. "It knocked you out. This lady wants to know if you're going to sue her."

Chet looked at the woman, then lay back down on the grass and put a hand to his forehead. "I think my brain is fried," he said dolefully. "How much can you sue for when your brain is fried?"

"For yours, about fifteen cents," Frank quipped.

Sitting up again, Chet gave him a reproachful look. He climbed to his feet and regarded the fence darkly.

"It's shut off now," the woman assured him. "Won't you come in the house while we discuss this?"

When they agreed, she unlocked the gate and led them inside. While they took seats in the living room, she went into the kitchen and returned with a tray of Cokes and a bowl of cookies.

"How are you feeling now?" she asked Chet as he reached for a handful of cookies."

"I think I'll live," he said.

It was apparent by the way he attacked the cookie bowl that he was fully recovered from the effects of the electrical shock. The woman looked relieved.

"Then you won't sue us?" she asked.

"I'll make a deal with you," Chet said. "You leave that fence switched off and I won't sue you."

"Oh, I will," she assured him. "I'm going to make my husband disconnect it."

The woman introduced herself as Mrs. Myra Steele, and the boys told her their names. Mrs. Steele explained that her husband was the famous movie writer Vincent Steele, and that he went to such great lengths to maintain his privacy because he was constantly being bothered by aspiring actors who wanted to break into the business.

"I can understand that," Chet said. "I'd like to be in the movies myself."

"What role would you play?" Joe asked. "A mountain?"

"He could play the body in murder mysteries," Frank suggested. "He put on a pretty good act outside."

"You fellows just don't appreciate real talent," Chet said in a patronizing tone.

Spotting an ashtray in the shape of a skull on a

nearby end table, he rose to his feet and picked it up. He stared down at it with a sad expression and intoned, "Alas, poor Yorick. I knew him well."

Mrs. Steele laughed along with the Hardys.

Joe said, "Maybe you knew poor Yorick, Chet, but you don't know your lines. "It goes, *'I knew him, Horatio,'* not *'I knew him well.'* Don't you remember our English teacher saying that was one of the most commonly misquoted lines in all literature?"

"I was out sick the day we studied *Hamlet,*" Chet said.

He set down the skull-like ashtray, returned to his seat, and took another cookie.

"Are you expecting your husband soon?" Frank asked Mrs. Steele.

"He won't be home tonight at all," she said. "He's away doing research for a script. Actually the script was all finished and the film is already being shot on location, but the director wanted Vincent to rewrite part of it."

She looked at the boys curiously. "Why did you come here? Did you want to speak to Vincent about something?"

Before Frank could answer, a car horn started to blow in front of the house. When it continued steadily, Frank stood up and walked over to the window. "Hey, that's our horn!" he exclaimed.

"Is somebody signaling for us?" Joe asked, moving to his brother's side.

"Nobody's out there!" Frank replied.

"Excuse us please, Mrs. Steele," Chet said. "We'd better go stop that awful noise."

When the woman nodded, Joe said, "We'll be right back."

The three hastened outside. By now it was beginning to turn dark. Frank reached the car first. He opened the door at the driver's side and banged the horn. It still continued to blow.

"There must be a short in it somewhere," Chet said.

Joe had already lifted the hood, and Frank got a screwdriver and a flashlight from the glove compartment. He handed them to Joe, who examined the wiring.

Meanwhile people appeared in the windows of several houses across the street, and one man came out to his front steps. "Stop that confounded noise, will you?" he shouted impatiently.

"We're trying to, sir," Chet replied.

Finally Joe said, "Look, this is no accidental short. Somebody attached a wire bridge across the connection." He removed the wire quickly and the horn stopped blowing.

Frank slammed the hood down as Joe returned the flashlight and the screwdriver to the glove compartment.

"Now who do you suppose did that?" asked Chet.

"There must be a practical joker living in this neighborhood," Joe said.

"Probably some kids," Frank declared.

Chet gingerly opened the gate and they started up the walk toward the front door of the Steele home.

Suddenly it dawned upon Frank that the drapes had been drawn tight over the front windows. Not even a crack of light could be seen from the interior.

Frank put his hand on the doorknob and tried to turn it. The door was locked. He pushed the bell, and heard it ring loud and clear, but there was no answer.

Impatiently Joe pressed the bell a couple of more times but to no avail.

"Maybe she's on the phone," Chet said.

"Could be," Frank agreed.

They waited a few more minutes, then Chet put his ear against the door. "I don't hear anything," he reported.

Frank wore a worried frown. "You know, fellows," he said, "I think we were deliberately faked out of the house by the guy who shorted our horn."

"But for what reason?" Chet asked.

"Maybe he wanted to duck in the back way as we went out the front," Frank replied.

"You mean a burglar?" Joe asked.

"Right," Frank said. He imagined the scene as

it might have taken place inside. Perhaps Mrs. Steele was bound and gagged and a thief was ransacking her house!

"The prowler might have closed the drapes, too," Joe said. "Come on. Let's see what's in back!"

All the drapes in the house had been drawn. The rear door was locked. Frank rang the bell while Chet pounded on the door.

"Mrs. Steele," Frank called out, "are you all right?"

Chet tried to open the kitchen window, but it was locked too. As he tried to force it, a cry came from inside the house.

"She really is in trouble!" Chet said. "Frank, do you think we ought to break in?"

"Mrs. Steele," Frank called again, as loud as he could.

"Listen," Joe said. "If someone's in there, he might try to escape by the front door. I'll go around to guard it."

But before he had a chance, the boys heard a car quietly drive up to the side of the house. Two doors slammed almost simultaneously, then a bright beam of light, like the eye of a giant cyclops, shone on the trio. It blinded them momentarily.

A deep voice said, "Hold it right there, you guys. Put your hands on the side of the house, quick!"

Frank started to go forward.

"Don't move or we'll shoot!"

Joe thought, "Accomplices of the fellow who's robbing the house!" His natural instinct was to resist, but the men might be armed and it could be a foolhardy move.

All three obeyed. Frank said, "What's your game?"

"Who are you?" Chet added.

"We're police officers. And you're under arrest!"

CHAPTER XII

The Sword Adalante

THE Bayporters placed their hands against the back wall of the house. One of the officers patted their bodies to see if they carried guns.

"They're clean," he growled to his companion. "All right, you can straighten up now."

Frank and Joe noticed that two more policemen had emerged from the car and were going into the house. Seconds later a floodlight over the garage door went on. Obviously they had switched it on from inside.

The two officers standing next to Frank and Joe holstered their guns. They wore the uniforms of deputy sheriffs.

The back door opened and Mrs. Steele stepped out.

"These are the ones!" she said. "Thanks for getting here so fast, Officers."

"Did you call the police about us?" Frank asked in astonishment.

"That's right!"

"But why?"

"You're thieves, aren't you?" the woman said tartly.

The boys looked at each other, then back at Mrs. Steele. "Where did you get that idea?" Joe inquired.

"While you were outside fixing your horn, the phone rang. It was a man. He wouldn't tell me his name, but he said to watch out for three young thieves who were working the neighborhood. He described you perfectly."

Frank said to the deputies, "Someone must be trying to get us in trouble. We were visiting with Mrs. Steele when our horn started blowing. We went to fix it and found it had been shorted on purpose. Probably the same person did it who phoned Mrs. Steele while we were outside!"

The deputy with the deep voice said, "Do you have any identification with you?"

"Certainly," Frank said, and all three handed over their driver's licenses.

After examining them, the deputy said, "I see you're all from Bayport. And two of you are named Hardy. Any relation to Fenton Hardy, the famous detective?"

"He's our father," Joe replied.

The deputy frowned at Mrs. Steele. "I don't

think the Hardy boys would steal anything, ma'am. You've heard of Fenton Hardy, haven't you?"

"Yes, of course. They didn't tell me they were his sons."

"Well, now that you know, how do you feel about it? We'll run them in if you want to sign a complaint."

Mrs. Steele hesitated. "Couldn't their identifications be faked? The man who phoned said they were thieves!"

Chet suddenly sat down on the back steps and put his hand to his forehead. "My brain's beginning to feel fried again," he said in a weak voice.

The deputy looked at him curiously. "What's wrong?" he asked.

Frank and Joe both realized Chet was acting. Joe said, "Aftereffect of the shock, I guess."

"What shock?"

Mrs. Steele said hurriedly, "I suppose the boys really are who they claim, and whoever called was just trying to cause a lot of trouble."

She gave Chet a fleeting glance and went on, "Perhaps I acted too hastily in phoning the sheriff. As you say, Fenton Hardy's sons wouldn't be thieves. Shall we just forget it? Will you boys come back inside?"

"What's wrong with him?" the deputy repeated.

Chet made a miraculous recovery. Standing up,

he said, "I had a little too much sun today, Officer, but I'm all right now. Let's go in, fellows."

The deputy still seemed suspicious, but there was nothing he could do except take Chet's explanation at face value. Since Mrs. Steele had decided to withdraw her charge, the officers left.

The woman switched off the light over the garage door and led the boys into the living room. She left them there while she carried the cookie bowl back to the kitchen to replenish it.

"You're some actor," Frank said to Chet. "Maybe you should be in the movies!"

"My fried brain sure got us invited back in the house fast, didn't it?" Chet said with a grin. "Mrs. Steele didn't want the deputies to know about that electrified fence."

"It can't be legal," Joe said. "These people would be in real trouble if the police found out about it."

"Who do you think shorted our horn and then phoned Mrs. Steele?" Chet asked. "Could it have been the same person who eavesdropped on us when we were talking to old Jimenez on the houseboat?"

"No," Frank replied. "That was Red Bowes, and he's in jail."

"How about Jimenez himself?" Chet inquired. "His great-uncle was a bandit. Maybe he's one, too!"

"That's silly," Joe said. "All that guy wants is to be left alone."

Mrs. Steele returned with the cookie bowl piled high and with fresh Cokes. When she had seated herself, she said to Chet, "Thanks for not telling the sheriff's men about our electric fence."

"I didn't want to get you in trouble," Chet said. "But you ought to disconnect it."

"I'll insist that my husband do it," she promised. "He's due home Sunday—tomorrow."

Frank asked, "What's the name of the movie your husband is working on?"

"It's working title is *The Sword Adalante,*" Mrs. Steele replied.

Chet nearly choked on his drink. When he recovered his breath, he sputtered, "Does he know where it is?"

"Where what is?" Mrs. Steele asked.

Joe, who was sitting next to Chet on the sofa, kicked his shin and said smoothly, "He means where is the movie being shot, don't you, Chet?"

"Uh—yes, that's what I meant," Chet said.

"Oh. The interiors are being done in a San Francisco studio. For the exteriors they're using a vineyard."

Frank asked, "What's the movie about?"

"It's based on the life of a legendary Swiss swordsman of the last century, Giovanni Russo. In the movie he is called something else, though, because there are living relatives who might object to the use of his name. I forget what they call him in the movie."

"What is the meaning of the movie's title?" Joe asked.

"The sword Adalante was a famous saber owned by Russo. In real life it was broken in a duel and lost many years ago. But in the movie this doesn't happen. The hero still has his sword at the end."

"We're interested in old swords," Frank said. "One of our teachers is writing a magazine article on the history of swords, and we're doing some research for him. Perhaps your husband can give us some information about this sword Adalante."

"I'm sure he'd be willing to," Mrs. Steele said. "It's the least he can do in return for your silence about the fence. Why don't you stop by here again tomorrow evening when he's home?"

The boys agreed to do this. After a few more minutes of conversation, they thanked her for the refreshments and left.

On their way to the car, Chet said, "I thought the reason we came here was to search the cellar for the guard end of that sword."

"I couldn't think of any excuse to ask to see the cellar," Frank said. "Why didn't you think of one?"

"My brain's fried, remember," Chet told him.

"You and Joe are supposed to be the smart ones."

"We'll get her husband to show it to us tomorrow," Joe put in. "I just had an idea about who might have shorted our horn and phoned Mrs. Steele."

"Who?" Frank asked.

"Harry Madsen."

"The bulldozer operator?" Chet asked. "Why would he want to do anything like that?"

"He threatened to get even with us."

In a thoughtful voice Frank said, "Could be." He looked around in all directions. "I don't see anyone lurking about, but then we didn't notice anybody before our horn was tampered with. Whoever it was may be watching us right now."

"Well," Chet decided, "it won't help to stand here. Let's go pick up a sack of hamburgers and head for the motel."

"Getting tired?" Joe queried. "All that sleuthing too much for you?"

"I almost lost my life!" Chet said indignantly.

He opened the rear door of the car and climbed in. Frank walked around to the driver's side and slid behind the wheel. As Joe got in next to him, his shoe came down on something soft and live that writhed beneath his foot and emitted a spine-chilling rattle!

CHAPTER XIII

A Blunt Warning

CAR doors burst open as all three boys jumped out. The dome light blinked on, revealing their uninvited guest. It was a thick rattlesnake, more than two feet long.

Hissing angrily, the reptile coiled and struck at Joe. But he slammed the door in time, severing the snake's head from the body.

"Whew!" he said, mopping his forehead with a handkerchief.

Chet leaned weakly on the fender. "You can say that again."

Frank came around to look at the headless rattler. "Somebody is starting to play rough," he muttered. "You can't pass this off as just a practical joke!"

"Seven rattles," Chet counted. "Doesn't that mean it was seven years old?"

"I think that's a myth," Joe replied. Lifting a

foot, he gingerly scraped the dead snake out into the gutter.

The boys got back into the car. Frank drove toward the bridge that led south off the island. In the rear-view mirror he had noted a pair of headlights that stayed about a half block behind them.

"Somebody's tailing us," Frank remarked.

The other two looked back. Chet said, "Must be whoever planted that snake. Let's stop and find out who it is."

"If it's that bank-robber gang, they're probably armed. We'd better shake them instead," Joe said.

"I agree with Joe," Frank decided.

He increased the Ford's speed. The car behind them started to go faster, too. By the time they reached the bridge, both were moving at sixty miles an hour.

Fortunately there was little traffic. They roared across to the next island and to the following bridge. Their tail stayed with them.

As they crossed the second bridge, the headlights of two approaching vehicles could be seen driving onto the other end. From the first one's size and height from the ground, the boys could tell that it was a large truck.

Passing on any of the bridges was against the law, but the driver of the vehicle behind the truck was impatient. Misjudging the speed of the Hardys' Ford, he started to swing around the truck.

All of a sudden headlights were glaring right into Frank's eyes. He hit the brakes hard. At the same instant the truck's tires squealed as its driver applied his air brakes. The reckless passer squeezed in by a hair's-breadth.

Frank was furious. "That idiot!" he said through clenched teeth.

Joe shook his head in disbelief.

Frank bore down on the accelerator again. Until they were out of the delta area, there was no way to shake the tailing car, because there was only one route to take.

On the outskirts of Stockton, however, Frank slowed in order to let the pursuing car get close behind them. Then he suddenly swung into a closed gas station. The other car shot on past.

As Frank circled around the pumps to swing back in the direction they had come from, his headlights shone briefly on the other car. Two men were in the front seat, but the boys could not make out who they were.

Their pursuers made a U-turn at the next intersection, but by then Frank had swung into a side street. After a series of random turns, he pulled over to the curb and cut his engine and lights.

"That should do the trick," Chet said, relieved.

"Let's wait and make sure," Joe suggested.

When several minutes had passed with no pursuer in sight, Frank drove to their motel.

It was a complex consisting of individual cabins. Frank pulled the Ford around behind theirs so it could not be seen from the road.

As they entered the cabin, Chet said, "We forgot to stop for hamburgers!"

"Doesn't anything make you forget food?" Joe asked. "A couple of killers are after us, remember?"

"Well, I don't want to die on an empty stomach," Chet complained.

"The motel restaurant is open all night. Go over there and get something if you want to."

After considering, Chet asked, "How do we know the killers aren't watching the restaurant?"

"We don't," Frank told him. "But it's unlikely they know where we're staying. They must have picked us up when we left the construction site after Joe's bout with Madsen. And we haven't been back here since, until now."

After weighing the possible danger of running into killers against satisfying his appetite, Chet decided to chance going to the restaurant. He returned with three hamburgers in a bag. Frank and Joe both declined, so Chet ate all three.

Even though they were fairly sure that their tails did not know where they were staying, the boys decided to take no chances. They divided the night into three watches, and each stayed awake for a couple of hours. Fortunately the night passed without incident.

The next morning after breakfast the boys decided to change cars. "That'll throw our tail off," Joe said.

They checked the yellow pages of the classified telephone directory and discovered that Stockton had a local branch of the car rental agency from which they had rented the Ford in San Francisco. It advertised twenty-four-hour service, seven days a week.

They drove down to the rental office, turned in their car, and selected a Chevrolet.

As they pulled out of the lot, Frank gave a grin of satisfaction. "That ought to throw those guys off our trail!" he said.

When they came back to the motel, they found a note under their door, requesting them to come to the office. Frank went.

The clerk said, "There was a phone call for either Frank or Joe Hardy. The man didn't tell me who he was, but he'll call back at eleven o'clock."

"How did anyone know we were here?" Frank wondered aloud, mystified.

"I don't know. He just asked if either of you were registered, and when I told him 'Yes,' he gave me the message."

"Thanks," Frank said and returned to the cabin.

When he relayed to the others what he had just heard, Joe said thoughtfully, "The man must have called all the motels in the neighborhood, asking if we were registered, until he hit pay dirt. Maybe we'd better move and check in somewhere else under false names."

"That's a good idea," Frank said. He looked at his watch. "It's five to eleven. So let's wait for the call before we leave."

The man phoned promptly a few minutes later, Frank answered, but held the receiver so that the others could hear, too.

A low, obviously disguised male voice said, "Is this one of the Hardy brothers?"

"Yes, this is Frank."

"If you value your lives, you'll get out of California before it's too late!"

There was a click as the man hung up.

Joe said ruefully, "Too bad we didn't have a recorder with us to tape the voice."

"We ought to pick up a portable job in case anything like this happens again," Frank suggested.

"Are any stores open on Sunday?" Chet wanted to know.

"There's a big shopping plaza a couple of blocks from the car rental office, and the parking lot was crowded when we went by," Joe said.

"It won't hurt to inquire," Frank said.

The boys checked into another motel a few blocks away. They let Chet register under his name, figuring that if the mysterious threatener called motels again, he would ask for the Hardys as he had before, not for Chet Morton.

Then they left for the shopping plaza. After they bought a pocket-sized tape recorder, they had lunch in a nearby restaurant. Chet suggested that since they were not due at the Steeles' house until that evening, they had time to check out the third wine storage building.

Frank grinned. "You're right on the ball, Chet! I was going to suggest that."

They drove across the various bridges to the island once owned by Giovanni Russo, and to the mountainous area at its north end.

They had no trouble finding Burns Mountain Road. It wound along about a mile before they came to a narrow gravel road leading off to the right. Chet pointed to a wooden sign that read: *Carson's Ski Lodge, 300 Yards.*

Frank parked in front of the building and they all got out. The lodge was at the base of a long slope, which obviously served as a ski run during the winter months. Their eyes followed the cable up the hill, where the lift ended at a low stone building.

"That must be the wine storage place," Joe said.

Frank nodded. "There's no other building in sight. But why would anyone store wine at the top of a hill?"

"Hey, guys!" Chet called out. "Look at this!"

"Vineyards might have covered all the slopes at one time," Chet reasoned. "But what a climb!"

"Too bad the lift isn't operating now," Joe said.

Chet noticed a sign posted on the porch of the lodge and went over to look at it.

"Hey, guys! Are we ever in luck!" he called out. "Look at this!"

Frank and Joe hastened over to read the notice. It said that the lift would be in service the following week. For a dollar people could ride up the mountaintop and enjoy the view.

"Bring the whole family on a picnic. Upper lodge will be open!" the sign invited.

"Now there's an idea just made to order for Chet," Joe said.

Chet ignored the gibe. "Do we have to climb now?" he inquired.

"I think we'd better wait," Frank replied. "No doubt the place up there is locked, so we couldn't get in anyhow. But it'll be open when the lift's running."

The boys drove back and had dinner at the same restaurant they had eaten the night before, then they drove to the screenwriter's house.

Chet glanced up and down the street, looking for anyone who might be a practical joker. But the street was empty.

When Frank rang the bell, Mrs. Steele came to

the door. She greeted them cordially and ushered them into the living room.

"My husband is in his den," she said. "Make yourselves comfortable while I get him."

"What do you suppose he's like?" Chet whispered after she had left.

"We'll soon find out," Frank said.

"I'll bet he looks like Ernest Hemingway," Joe said. "You know, very distinguished, like writers are supposed to look."

A few moments later footsteps sounded and Mrs. Steele returned. Behind her was a tall, thin, gray-haired man. A yellow scarf with tiny black polka dots was knotted around his neck.

Frank stared at the man's face in utter astonishment.

"Professor Von Stolk!" he blurted out.

CHAPTER XIV

The Cellar Museum

THE man reacted as if he had walked into a brick wall. "You're—you're the boy who was talking to June at the college library," he said limply to Frank.

Mrs. Steele spoke up. "Why did you call him Professor Von Stolk? This is my husband—Vincent Steele."

"Something needs a lot of explaining," Frank said. "Your husband called himself Von Stolk when I saw him the first time." In afterthought he added, "You used the same initials when you changed your name, didn't you, Mr. Steele?"

Turning to his wife, Vincent Steele said in a placating tone, "Don't let this upset you, my dear. I hired a young woman to do some research for me."

His wife looked at him slit-eyed. "Yes, go on!"

"I knew if I told her who I really was, she and

all her friends would be plaguing me to get them into the movies."

"Oh, that again," she said. "Now I understand."

To the boys she said apologetically, "Vincent is so publicity shy. You can see why, can't you?"

She introduced the boys by name and the screenwriter formally offered a hand to each.

Then Frank asked, "Was it you or June Fall who removed four pages from the *Master of the Vineyards* book, Mr. Steele?"

"Neither," he replied, looking uncomfortable. "They were already missing." Suddenly he became belligerent, and fired a burst of questions at the boys.

"Why are you interrogating me like this? What did you come to my house for? What business is it of yours that I go to the library?"

Frank realized that perhaps they had pushed their case too fast. Nothing would be gained by antagonizing the writer, even though he was a suspect. In a calm voice Frank said, "Mr. Steele, we came here to ask your assistance."

"What assistance? I don't even know you."

"It's about your home. It was once a wine cellar."

"That's right. How did you find out?"

"From an old map."

The Steeles looked confused. Joe felt sorry that the writer's wife had become involved in the deepening mystery. Would Frank tell them about the sword? Or would he sidestep the real intent of their visit?

When his brother hesitated, Joe said, "You can't blame us for becoming suspicious when you use two names, Mr. Steele. And about those pages missing from the library book, weren't you showing them to Harry Madsen at the construction site last evening?"

Steele frowned. "Were you spying on me then?"

"Only by accident," Joe replied. "We didn't expect to see you there."

"What were you doing there?"

"We were watching the bulldozer operator," Frank put in. "He had been causing us some trouble. But you haven't answered the question."

"Look, you've got it all wrong," Steele said with a sigh. "They weren't the pages from that book. I have a hobby of collecting vineyard implements. For some time I've been meaning to go through that building at the housing construction site which was once used to store wine. But I never got around to it."

He stood up, left the living room, and came back with two sheets of paper.

"These are sketches of a particular type of barrel I've been looking for. When I heard that the wine storage place was going to be razed yesterday, I called the contractor."

"And he promised to postpone the bulldozing," Joe said.

"Correct. As long as I would pay for the expense. I met with Madsen last night, showed him the sketches, took a look in the building, but did not find what I wanted."

He put the sketches on a table. "Come," he offered. "I will show you the museum."

He led the way to a central hallway and opened a door to a narrow stone stairway leading downward. Flicking a light switch at the top, he descended. Chet went second, then Frank and Joe. Mrs. Steele remained in the living room.

The cellar had been converted into a museum. The rooms were similar in shape to those of the other wine storage building, except there were no cobwebs and the interiors were clean and well illuminated by overhead lights.

"Quite an exhibit," Frank said, looking around in surprise.

The rooms were crammed with artifacts of grape farming and wine making. There were wooden racks, ancient hand-blown bottles, wine presses, casks of various sizes and shapes, wooden aging vats and many other items.

At the rear of one room the boys spotted an ancient, ornately carved oaken door.

"What's in there?" Joe asked.

"Nothing," Steele replied. "It's merely an empty storage room. We don't use it. Shall we go upstairs again?"

When they returned to the living room, Steele apologized to Chet for the electric fence incident, and thanked the boys for not getting him in trouble with the police.

"Are you fully recovered?" he asked solicitously.

"Except for a little dizzy spell now and then," Chet replied. "But I don't think it's anything serious."

Vincent Steele said worriedly, "I'd be glad to pay for a doctor if you want to see one."

"I'll be all right," Chet assured him. Then he had an inspiration. "There's something else you could do for me, though."

"What's that?"

"Get me into the movies!"

The man winced slightly. In a resigned voice he said, "I might have known. Do you have any acting experience?"

"No, but I'm willing to start at the bottom."

"That would be as an extra," Steele said. "I might be able to arrange that. This coming Tuesday we'll start shooting some exteriors and we'll need a lot of extras as grape pickers. If you could get there at six in the morning, I think I can fix it for all three of you to get jobs."

"We could sure use the money," Joe said. "We're running pretty low. Where do we report?"

"We're on location at a farm called the San

Mathilde Vineyard a little over a hundred miles southeast of here on Highway 99. It's just beyond Fresno. You'll see the sign."

"Whom do we ask for?" Frank inquired.

"Jason Andrews, the casting chief."

Mrs. Steele changed the subject. "The main reason the boys came here tonight is to ask you about the sword Adalante."

For the second time that night, Steele was brought up short. He stared from one boy to another in dumbfounded silence.

"A teacher of theirs is doing a magazine article on the history of swords," Mrs. Steele explained. "The boys are helping with the research. I happened to mention the title of your current movie and they thought their teacher might use something about the sword in his article."

"Oh," Vincent Steele said with evident relief. "Actually I don't know a great deal about the sword. It was broken in a duel and lost many years ago. The tip end eventually was found, and now is in the possession of Russo's family in Switzerland. The guard end was never recovered."

A phone on a small table next to Mrs. Steele rang. She answered it.

"Someone's asking for either Frank or Joe Hardy," she said.

Frank looked perplexed. They had told no one where they were going.

Taking out the pocket recorder, Joe said, "I guess we ought to tape this."

He took the phone from Mrs. Steele, switched on the recorder, and held it close to the receiver. As Frank and Chet crowded around him, he said, "Joe Hardy speaking."

"This is a warning. Get out of California if you want to continue breathing!" a disguised voice said. Then there was a click as the caller hung up.

Joe winked at Chet for silence and Frank, too, betrayed no reaction.

"Anything wrong?" Mrs. Steele asked in a motherly tone.

When Joe shook his head, the woman continued, "Why did you tape the call?"

"It's our hobby," Frank said. "Well, I guess we'd better be going."

The boys thanked the Steeles for their hospitality and departed. On the way back to their motel, they discussed the second threat.

"Probably the same goon as before," Chet said.

Joe disagreed. "His voice was not as deep as the first man's," he said.

Frank, who was driving, asked, "Any sign of a tail?"

"No," Joe replied. "I've been watching ever since we left."

"What do you think about Steele?" Chet wanted to know. "He looks clean to me. His explanations seemed okay."

Frank and Joe were dubious.

Joe said, "He was glib enough, but there's something about that man I don't trust."

Frank had a more specific reason. "Did you notice," he said, "that Steele never pressed us for the real reason for our first visit?"

"Searching for the broken blade, you mean?" Chet said.

"Right."

"I never thought of that," Joe stated. "Frank asked for his assistance at one point, and Steele never came back to it."

"He did that on purpose," Frank said. "Didn't want to raise the issue. I think he suspects we're looking for the Adalante."

"Then we've got to be careful of him," Chet said.

"Very careful," Frank agreed.

When they reached the motel, Chet said, "Are we going to move again?"

"We've already paid for tonight," Frank pointed out. "And we're running pretty low on money. Let's stay here and stand watch again."

Joe played back the taped conversation. The caller's voice came over strong and clear.

"That's good enough to make a spectrograph," Frank said with satisfaction. "Tomorrow we'll run into San Francisco and use the police department's machine."

Again they divided the night into three shifts,

but it passed peacefully. Next morning they checked out of the motel and drove to San Francisco.

Chief of Detectives Henry Copeland was glad to see them. They had no trouble getting permission to use the spectrograph. Frank made three voiceprints. They left one with Copeland, mailed the second to Chief Collig, and kept the third.

Instead of returning to Stockton, they decided to drive to Fresno so that they would be near the movie location Tuesday morning. Again there was no sign of a tail, but they took no chances. In their Fresno motel they repeated their night watch. Nothing happened.

Promptly at six the next morning they arrived at the San Mathilde Vineyard. It consisted of several thousand acres. There was a Spanish-style hacienda in which the owner and his family lived, but the grape pickers were housed in a row of tar paper shacks. Row after row of grapevines stretched off into the distance.

A number of trailers were parked near the workers' shacks. These were being used as dressing rooms for actors. Several Nissen huts had also been set up to serve as offices. One of them had a sign on its door: *Casting Office*.

The boys went in and found a thin, harried-looking man seated behind a desk. He glanced up from the magazine he was reading.

"Mr. Andrews?" Frank asked.

"Yes, yes," the man replied somewhat testily, as if he were annoyed by the interruption. "What do you want?"

"I'm Frank Hardy, this is my brother Joe and our buddy Chet Morton. Mr. Steele told us to report to you for extra work."

The casting chief squinted his eyes as if searching his memory. "Oh yes," he said. "Vincent mentioned it." He looked the boys up and down.

"You'll need some old clothes," he added, "because you'll be cast as pickers."

"Where do we get 'em?" Chet inquired.

"Maybe you can borrow some from the vineyard workers. Report back tomorrow at six."

"Tomorrow?" Frank said. "Mr. Steele told us shooting was supposed to start today."

"It was, but there's been a delay."

The boys looked disappointed and were about to leave when Joe turned to the movie man. "There's nothing seriously wrong, I hope," he said.

"Serious enough," Andrews grunted.

The Hardys' curiosity was piqued.

"Can you tell us what's wrong, sir?" Frank asked.

"Ettore's been injured."

"Ettore?" Frank said, puzzled.

Jason Andrews seemed impatient that they did not know whom he was talking about.

"The fencing master who acts as the star's double," he explained. "Ettore Rossi."

"You mean Ettore Russo?" Chet said weakly.

"Of course not. Trouble is, you young people don't listen. I said Ettore Rossi!"

CHAPTER XV

Star-Struck!

THE Hardys and Chet were amazed at the similarity of names between Hollywood's fencing master and their own coach.

Frank said, "We know a fencing master named Ettore Russo. Is this man a Swiss?"

"No. He's an Italian." Andrews replied. "Ettore has been a stuntman for years. Also drives race cars."

"Where do we find Mr. Rossi?" Frank asked. "We'd like to talk with him."

"In trailer four," the casting chief said.

As they started out, the door opened and a beautiful blond woman dressed in a Spanish costume came in. The boys stepped aside to let her pass.

The woman gave them a dazzling smile as she swept by.

"Do you know who that was?" Chet said in an awed voice, when they were out of the office.

"Sure." Frank grinned. "Brenda White. She must be starring in the picture."

Chet halted and stared at his two friends. "Aren't you impressed?"

"Of course we are," Joe replied. "She's very beautiful. But we're not going to go ape over her."

"You guys have no feelings," Chet retorted. "Don't you realize we're going to be working in the same picture as Brenda White?"

"She won't even notice us," Frank said. "We're only going to be extras."

They moved on to trailer number four. When Frank knocked on the door, a strong voice called, "Come in!"

Inside they found a black-haired man in a half-reclining position on a bunk with a pillow under his back.

"Mr. Rossi?" Frank asked.

"Yes. What can I do for you?"

Frank introduced himself and the others. Then he said, "We've just been hired as extras. Mr. Andrews told us you were hurt, so we dropped by to cheer you up. What happened?"

"A practical joke," the stuntman said ruefully. "Someone sprayed banana oil on the trailer floor while I was asleep. When I got up this morning, I slipped and wrenched my back."

"That wasn't a very funny joke," Chet commented.

"None of them are," Ettore Rossi said grimly. "If I ever find out who's behind all this, I'll teach him what's funny and what isn't."

Joe said, "Things like this have happened before?"

"Twice. Once the brakes on my racing car were tampered with, almost causing a crash. Another time a sandbag was dropped from an overhead catwalk on an interior set, nearly braining me."

"They don't sound like practical jokes!" Frank exclaimed. "It looks as if somebody's out to kill you!"

All at once the Italian's expression became withdrawn. "I shouldn't be talking about it anyway," he said. "Mr. Zeller told me not to."

"Who's Mr. Zeller?" Joe asked.

"The director of the movie."

"Why doesn't he want you to discuss it?"

"He's afraid it'll give the picture bad publicity. He's having a quiet investigation made."

There was a knock on the door and a short, fat man came in. He looked worried. Rossi introduced him to the boys as movie director Gene Zeller.

After shaking hands, Mr. Zeller said, "I just learned of your mishap, Ettore. How long will you be laid up this time?"

"At least two or three days, according to the

doctor. You'll have to get someone else to double in the fencing scenes you planned to shoot today and tomorrow."

"Where?" the director said, wrinkling his brow. "There's no one around here who knows how to fence. I'll have to send either to Hollywood or San Francisco. By the time we locate somebody you'll be up and around again."

Frank said, "We know how to fence."

The director looked him up and down. "You're about the same height and weight as Douglas Clark, our leading man. Makeup can take care of other physical differences. Are you good at fencing?"

Joe answered for him. "He sure is."

"Any experience with sabers?" Rossi asked.

"We know all three weapons," Joe replied. "Saber, foil, and épée."

"But these will be real sabers, not fencing sabers," Rossi told him. "Of course the points and blades will be dulled, but you'll wear no masks or gloves. Before the camera your performance has to look like real dueling. You have to be pretty expert not to hurt your opponent or get hurt yourself."

"I'm sure my brother and I could put on a good act," Frank said. "We've fenced together so often. I don't know how it would be with some stranger, though."

"Your brother could work as your opponent in the scenes we shoot today—and tomorrow—if you're good enough," the director said. "It involves a duel with a bandit who doesn't appear in any other scenes."

"Gene, why don't you get a pair of sabers and let them show what they can do right outside my window?" Rossi suggested.

"Good idea," Zeller replied and called a prop man. He instructed him to bring the weapons.

Soon the man returned with the sabers. They were thirty-four and a half inches long, the tournament length to which the Hardys were accustomed.

After hefting them, Frank and Joe were sure they could handle the bout.

"Okay, go to it," Zeller said.

The boys took up positions outside the window next to Rossi's bunk.

"We'd better warn each other what to expect before each attack," Frank suggested. "This way the defendant will know what type of parry to make."

"Right," Joe said. "On guard!"

"Beat attack!" Frank called out, striking Joe's blade aside.

Joe parried. "Pressure glide."

Parrying, Frank called, "Envelopment."

They continued to attack and parry in turn, the

blades clashing and sliding against each other in the cadence of a deadly dance. The audition soon drew a crowd of spectators.

Neither boy attempted to score, knowing it would have drawn blood, but their performance was colorful and convincing. When they finally paused after several minutes of intricate swordplay, the audience applauded loudly.

"They'll do fine," Rossi called out. "Sign 'em up, Gene."

"That solves that problem," the director said with relief. "I guess we'll be able to shoot today after all."

While the swordplay had been going on, Chet kept glancing around in the hope of spotting one of the film's stars. But neither Douglas Clark nor Brenda White appeared.

Gradually it penetrated Chet's consciousness that every time he looked over the crowd, the shadowy figure of a man seemed to be just fading out of his range of vision.

When he deliberately looked for the man, the figure immediately drifted behind one of the trailers. Chet noticed that he wore a peaked cap pulled low over his face.

Was he one of the fellows who had been tailing them? Chet wondered. Or the one who had phoned Steele's house and threatened them?

Pushing his way through the crowd, Chet circled around to the spot where he had lost sight of the shadowy figure. He was just in time to see the man duck behind the next trailer.

Chet followed. The man quickened his pace and disappeared around the far end. When Chet ran around the corner, he saw the trailer's door close.

"I've got him cornered!" Chet muttered. He climbed the steps and flung open the door.

Instantly a yapping ball of fur attacked his ankles, nipping with tiny sharp teeth.

"Go away, dog!" Chet commanded. He backed through the door, tumbled down the steps, and sat in the dust. Someone scooped up the furious little Pomeranian in time to prevent it from leaping at Chet, who looked up ruefully.

Brenda White stood in the doorway, clutching the tiny dog!

"Oh, I'm sorry," she said contritely. "Did naughty little Fifi hurt you?"

Examining his ankles and finding no trace of blood, Chet said, "No, ma'am." Embarrassed, he got to his feet and brushed himself off. "It was my fault, Miss White. I shouldn't have burst in that way. But I was chasing a man and thought he ran in there."

"Into my trailer?" the movie star said with a tinkling little laugh. "There's no one here but me and Fifi. We just came in ourselves."

"Yes, ma'am," Chet said. "Sorry I disturbed you."

"It's all right," Brenda White said. "I'm glad you're not hurt." She closed the door.

Chet circuited all of the other trailers, the Nissen huts, and the grape pickers' tar-paper shacks, but he failed to spot the man wearing the cap. By the time he got back to the Hardys, their fencing demonstration was over. The audience had dispersed and the director explained to Frank and Joe what the scene would be.

"You'll get a better idea when you read the script," he said. "Before you go to Wardrobe for your costumes and to Makeup, stop by Production and get a copy of exterior scene four from the script girl."

"Yes, sir," Frank said.

They started toward the Nissen hut containing the Production Office. Chet fell in at their side.

Zeller called after them, "The script girl's name is Laura."

Frank and Joe waved acknowledgment.

Chet said, "Some man in a cap is sneaking around spying on somebody—maybe us. I tried to catch up with him to see what he looked like, but he got away."

"Think it's one of our tails?" Joe asked.

Chet shrugged. "He realized I was after him and took off like a scared rabbit."

They reached the Production Office and went in. Frank told the brunette at the reception desk that they had been sent by Mr. Zeller to see Laura, the script girl.

"In there," the receptionist said, pointing to a door. The boys entered and saw a woman sitting at a desk with her back to them.

Hearing their steps, she glanced over her shoulder.

Frank and Joe stopped dead in their tracks. "Mom!" they exclaimed in unison.

The script girl was their mother, Laura Hardy!

"But—but you're supposed to be at the Grand Canyon!" Joe said as Mrs. Hardy rose to hug her sons.

CHAPTER XVI

Weird Attackers

STUNNED by the discovery of his mother on a California movie location, Frank's next thought was of his father. "Where's Dad?" he asked.

As he spoke, a door marked *Maintenance Department* just beyond Laura Hardy's desk opened and Fenton Hardy stepped out. He was carrying a cap in his hand.

Joe rushed over to put an arm around Mr. Hardy's shoulder, while Frank grinned at the famous detective.

"Dad, what's going on here?" Joe asked.

Mr. Hardy smiled at them without the least sign of surprise. But before he could reply, Chet exclaimed in amazement, "That was you I was chasing, Mr. Hardy! Why didn't you let me know?"

"I was testing your running ability, Chet." Mr. Hardy looked at his sons. "Tell me, what are you doing here?"

"After you, Dad," Frank insisted.

Fenton Hardy explained that he and his wife had met Zeller at the Grand Canyon, where the director had begged him to investigate the attempts on Ettore Rossi's life.

"Gene was so upset that I agreed," Mr. Hardy said, "and we cut our vacation short. As a cover-up I was hired as a maintenance man and your mother is here as a script girl."

"That's a neat idea," Chet stated. "You get to meet all the important stars!"

Joe laughed. "Mom, Chet's ga-ga about Miss White."

"She's gorgeous," Chet said dreamily.

Frank changed the subject. "I was wondering about those planned accidents plaguing Mr. Rossi. Maybe the people responsible for them have the wrong man. It could be that they're really after Ettore Russo."

"Your fencing instructor in Bayport?" the detective asked in surprise. "Why would anyone be after him?"

The boys explained about their maestro being one of the grandsons of Giovanni Russo; about the will written on the sword Adalante; and how Russo had paid their way to California to search for the guard end of the broken blade.

When they finished their story, Mr. Hardy said thoughtfully, "Frank, your deduction is sound. That must be the explanation. Ettore Russo's greedy cousin in Switzerland probably hired these criminals to dispose of him, and they picked the wrong man because of the similarity in names. Besides, I remember Russo telling me that he lived in California before opening the school in Bayport."

The boys told their father about the Bayport bank robbery and the theft of his voiceprint file. But he already knew, because he had been in touch with Chief Collig. However, the capture of Red Bowes was news to him. Frank and Joe related everything else that had happened since their arrival in San Francisco.

"Oh dear!" Mrs. Hardy said. "I'm glad you weren't hurt."

Mr. Hardy said, "It sounds to me as though the answer to all this lies in Stockton, not here. You can't leave Zeller in a spot after agreeing to act in those sword-fighting scenes, but as soon as your work in the movie is finished, we'll all go to Stockton."

"How about Mr. Rossi?" Mrs. Hardy asked. "Shouldn't you stay here to protect him from danger?"

"He won't be in any if we let his tormentors know they're bugging the wrong man," Mr. Hardy replied. "I'll suggest to Gene that he issue a publicity release about his stuntman. Mention can be made that his name is very similar to Giovanni Russo's grandson."

"The newspapers would like that," Laura Hardy said.

"Not to mention radio and TV," Frank added. "It's a good feature story, and the goons will be sure to hear it."

"It won't place Mr. Russo in any danger either," his father went on, "because he's out of the country."

Mrs. Hardy smiled at her sons. "How's your money holding out, incidentally?"

"They're almost as broke as I am," Chet volunteered.

Frank and Joe frowned at him. "We're earning plenty for our movie work," Joe said. "We don't need any money."

"I'm going to see Gene about that publicity release," Mr. Hardy declared. "Well talk about Stockton later."

Joe said, "Come on, Frank. We'd better get out of here, too. We have to go to Wardrobe, then to Makeup, and we're due on the set in an hour."

Mrs. Hardy gave them a copy of the exterior scene script and they left with their father.

Chet lingered behind to talk to Mrs. Hardy. She opened her purse and took out some bills.

"Put this away in case of emergency," she said.

"Thanks, Mrs. Hardy," he replied with a grateful grin. "If we don't need it, I'll return the cash in Bayport."

The sword-fighting scene went well. Zeller told

Frank and Joe that they would be needed for a similar scene the next morning. After that they would be through.

That afternoon the vineyard scene was shot. The boys played grape pickers. They had borrowed suitable clothing from some of the workers on the farm, who had all been hired as extras, too.

By noon the next day they were finished and had been paid. Mr. and Mrs. Hardy took them to lunch at the Golden Gate Restaurant near the vineyard, where all the motion-picture personnel ate. During the meal they discussed their next move.

"I think we'd better drive to Stockton separately," Mr. Hardy said. "If your enemies pick up the trail again, there's no point in their knowing about Mother and me."

"Suppose we meet somewhere in Stockton for dinner tonight?" Joe suggested.

"All right. Where?"

"Swanson's Drive-in Restaurant on the north side would be a good place," Chet said. "We could park our cars next to each other and talk without being overheard."

It was decided to meet at Swanson's at six o'clock that evening.

The boys went to Stockton and checked into a motel near the restaurant. Promptly at six they drove to the drive-in's parking lot and waited.

A carhop had just taken their orders when a

black Plymouth slid into the next spot. In it were Mr. and Mrs. Hardy.

Mr. Hardy did not even say hello until their order was taken, too. Then he said, "Any sign of a tail on you?"

"We didn't see any," Joe replied.

"Where are you staying?"

"At the Delta Motel."

"We're at the Northside Plaza," Mr. Hardy said. "When do you plan to search that old wine storage building at Carson's Ski Lodge?"

"According to the sign they had up last week," Frank said, "the lift should be in operation till eight o'clock. So let's do it right now."

"I'm all for that," Mr. Hardy agreed. Turning to his wife, he said, "I'll go in the boys' car, Laura, and you can drive back to the motel in this one."

"All right, Fenton."

When they had finished eating and paid their checks, Mr. Hardy slipped into the back seat of the Chevrolet with Chet. Mrs. Hardy moved over to take the wheel of the Plymouth.

At that moment a green Buick drove in on the other side of her car.

"Oh, oh," Frank said in a low voice. "There's Harry Madsen and his friend Amos Cain."

After a quick look, Joe and Chet averted their faces so that the pair would not recognize them. Joe whispered, "Don't back out yet, Mom. Wait until we leave."

Mrs. Hardy nodded.

Frank started the engine and pulled out. Joe and Chet kept their heads turned, but Mr. Hardy got a good look at the two men as Frank drove off.

"I'm pretty sure they weren't tailing you," Mr. Hardy said. "It must have been a coincidence that they came in."

"Probably," Chet agreed. "It's a popular place."

Nevertheless Frank kept one eye on the rear-view mirror whenever he could, and the others watched out, too. But there was no sign of pursuit.

Soon they reached the ski lodge. No one was in sight. The place was no longer boarded up, but it was closed for the day. Frank parked in front of the lodge and they all got out.

Joe looked at his watch. It was a few minutes after seven, and still light. "They must have closed early," he remarked.

Pointing to the stone building atop the mountain, Frank said to his father, "That's it up there, Dad."

They went to look at the chair-lift engine. To their surprise it was not locked. After examining it for a few moments, Fenton Hardy started it.

Joe got a flashlight from the car and thrust it under his belt. Then he and Frank took seats on the lift. Mr. Hardy shifted the engine into gear, and with a slight jerky motion the boys started the long trip upward.

They rose higher and higher over the slope, until halfway up they were more than thirty feet above the grade. Then the distance to the ground diminished as they neared the peak.

They stepped off the lift only a dozen yards from the oaken door of the stone building. Their double seat continued on, took a hundred and eighty degree turn around a stanchion, and headed back down the hill on the moving cable.

Frank tried the door of the lodge. It was locked. They walked around and discovered that a window had been broken.

"Somebody's been in here!" said Frank.

"I wonder how long ago," Joe mused.

"It must be since the place closed today," Frank replied. "Otherwise the operators would have noticed the break and boarded it up."

Joe snapped his fingers. "I'll bet that's why the lift engine wasn't padlocked! Whoever broke in here, probably busted the lock and used the lift to get up and down again."

"Well," Frank said, "as long as the window's broken, we might as well take advantage of it." He climbed inside, careful to avoid the jagged pieces of glass jutting from the frame. Joe followed.

As they stepped onto the floor, Frank grabbed Joe's arm and put a finger to his lips.

"What's the matter?" Joe whispered.

Frank sniffed. "Smell the smoke?"

"From a cigarette!"

"Right. Someone's in here!"

The young sleuths tingled with a mixture of fright and excitement. If somebody had just preceded them, why? How many were there? And where were they hiding?

As the odor of cigarette tobacco drifted out through the broken window, the boys surveyed the dim interior. The room they were in was small and rimmed with benches. At one end was a potbellied stove for the skiers in winter.

In addition to the locked front door there was another door. What lay beyond? they wondered. Somebody was there, they felt sure.

After a whispered consultation the boys decided to climb out, circle the building, and spy into the mysterious room from a window on the far side.

Frank had one foot through the broken windowpane when a bloodcurdling yell sounded behind them.

Immobilized by surprise, the Hardys froze for a moment, then turned to see two weird faces, grotesquely flattened by nylon stocking masks. One man was tall and thin, the other burly.

The tall man held a pistol in his hand. "Look what we've caught, Homer!" he said.

"The Hardy boys! What a catch, Charlie!"

The voices sounded familiar in spite of the slightly muffled tone.

"Pretty far from New Jersey, aren't you?" Frank asked.

For a moment there was stunned silence, then Joe delivered his shot. "You won't find any spectrographs here, Charlie!"

With that the men ripped off their masks. "Okay, so you recognize us," Charlie said. "Little good it'll do you." He waved his gun at the boys. "Cross your hands in front of you!" he ordered, and pulled two cords from his pocket.

CHAPTER XVII

Treasure in the Dust

FROM down below, Mr. Hardy and Chet watched Frank and Joe climb through the broken window. Suddenly the sound of a breaking twig made them turn around.

A squat, muscular man had stepped out from behind the ski lodge. He pointed a revolver at them.

"Up with your hands!" he ordered.

Mr. Hardy and Chet obeyed. Commanding them to turn their backs, the man checked them for weapons.

"Who are you and what do you want?" Mr. Hardy asked.

"Never mind," the man replied. "Just keep quiet!"

He kept his gun on them while he periodically peered up at the mountaintop. Several minutes passed, then four people emerged from the stone building. Frank and Joe were first, their wrists bound together in front of them.

Charlie got on the lift with Frank.

"All right," the squat man with the gun told Mr. Hardy. "Bring the next seat into position so the other two can get on."

Perspiration stood out on the detective's forehead as he obeyed. When everyone was on the lift, he started the engine again, furiously trying to think of a way to escape.

When the four were halfway down, the cable stopped moving. Mr. Hardy attempted to get the lift operating again, but could not.

"What's the matter?" the gunman asked gruffly.

"Don't know. Give me a minute to check it out."

Up on the lift, meanwhile, Homer and Charlie became impatient. "If he can't get it going," Charlie called to his accomplice, "we'll have to reduce the weight and throw these kids overboard."

"You can't do that!" Frank cried out.

"Oh no?" Homer sneered. "It would save us a lot of trouble. Let's not waste any time!"

He lifted Joe's safety bar and pushed him off the seat. Frantically the boy grasped the bottom of the chair and hung on for dear life. His captor pulled out a gun and smashed it on Joe's fingers. Joe winced in pain. Desperately he swung one foot around and kicked his adversary in the shin.

All at once the ski lift started moving again. While Homer grabbed at his legs with both hands, Joe quickly pulled himself back into the seat.

As the lift neared the base of the hill, Frank and Joe saw their father and Chet held at bay by the thug.

Homer chortled, "Kell's got the kids' old man and the fat boy!"

When they reached the ground and had stepped down, Charlie turned to Kell. "What now?" he asked.

"You take the two boys with you," Kell replied. "I'll follow with these two birds in their car."

Frank and Joe were marched a distance from the lodge to a small parking area concealed from the road by trees and bushes. They were forced into the back seat of a dark sedan. Homer slid behind the wheel and Charlie climbed in next to him. Seconds later they pulled out and roared away.

Meanwhile, Kell ordered Mr. Hardy and Chet into the front of the Chevy. "You drive!" he growled at the detective and took his position in the back seat, gun trained on his captives.

Slowly Mr. Hardy eased the car onto the gravel road.

Joe hung on for dear life!

Chet turned halfway around. "You think you're real smart, eh?" he said, fuming.

"Oh, shut up, Fatso," Kell replied. He leaned forward, and rested his gun hand on the back of the boy's seat. "You're so stupid you walked right into our arms!"

"You mean you knew we were coming?" Chet demanded.

"Naw. But you made so much noise before the two kids even got on the lift that we had plenty of warning. We—"

Suddenly Chet whirled and smashed his fist into the man's ear. The gun dropped on the front seat. But Kell instantly recovered his wits. He hit Chet in the side of his neck, opened the back door in a lightning move, and threw himself out of the car.

Before Mr. Hardy had skidded to a halt and taken up pursuit, he had melted away in the darkness.

Chet, who had been stunned for a few moments, looked dejectedly at the detective as he came back to the car. "Sorry about that, Mr. Hardy. I was hoping we could reverse roles and take this jerk to headquarters!"

Mr. Hardy put a hand on the boy's shoulder. "Listen, Chet, you were great. You may have saved both our lives!"

"Now we'll have to rescue Frank and Joe." Chet sighed.

"Right. Only we haven't any idea where they are!"

Frank and Joe were in the back seat of the sedan, unconscious. A slight odor of chloroform hung in the air.

An hour later Joe awakened. He found himself on his back in pitch darkness, his hands still bound in front of him. The air was chilly. It felt as though he was lying on loosely packed dirt.

The sound of deep breathing came from his right. As he sat up, he felt the flashlight still tucked under his belt. Their captors must not have noticed it. He took it out and flicked it on.

Playing it around, he realized they were in a cavelike chamber about twenty feet across. The walls and the domed ceiling were of solid stone. The floor, as he had suspected, was dirt. The only entrance was blocked by a heavy oaken door.

The deep breathing had been coming from Frank who was lying next to Joe. Now it quieted. Frank opened his eyes and sat up.

"Where are we?" he asked.

Shrugging, Joe said, "I haven't the faintest idea. Let's get these ropes off our wrists."

Setting down the flashlight, he struggled to his feet. It was difficult without the use of his hands.

Frank managed to get up, too. He worked at his brother's bonds until he got them loose, then Joe untied him.

He picked up the light again and shone it on the door. Frank tried it and found it locked. He threw his weight against it, but it did not budge. It was far too thick to break down.

Joe shone the light on the hinges. They were made of thick leather, rutted and dry from old age. These were attached to the door by huge brass studs.

"Wow!" Joe said. "These hinges were made to last an eternity."

"Don't say that," Frank muttered. "We might be in here that long."

The boys felt the thick leather. Joe said, "If we had a knife, we could cut through them."

"But we don't have one," Frank said. "Any other suggestions?"

Joe shone the flashlight all around. "The dirt on the floor is fairly loose, Frank," he said. "Maybe we could dig our way under the door with our hands."

"It's worth a try," Frank conceded.

Joe put the light on the ground, pointing at the door. Both boys dropped to their knees. They began to scoop handfuls of dirt away from the door's base. Joe worked furiously. Under the first layer of soil, the earth was powdery dry. Particles filled the air, making them cough violently.

"Joe! Not so fast. Don't scatter the dust!" Frank warned.

They tied handkerchiefs over their nostrils and

Joe dug more cautiously. But the bottom of the door was so far down in the earth, it would take considerable time to make an opening large enough to crawl through.

After they had excavated a hole of about six inches, Frank's hand touched something solid.

"Hey, Joe, what's this?" Pushing the dirt away from the object on either side, he pulled out a rusty blade about a foot and a half long. At one end was a moldy saber handle.

Excitedly Joe focused the light on his brother's find. "Holy crow! It can't be!" he exclaimed. The letters A-N-T-E were dimly visible on the blade.

"It's the sword Adalante!" Joe cried.

"Is the will engraved on it?" Frank asked eagerly.

After peering at the blade, Joe said, "We'll have to wait until we get it in a better light. And we'll have to clean it up a little. It's pretty tarnished. Probably we'll be able to see the engraving after we shine it up a bit."

"Is the blade sharp enough to cut those hinges?" Frank asked.

Joe tested it with his thumb. "I think so."

He began sawing at the lower hinge while Frank held the light. It took ten minutes to penetrate the hardened leather, but eventually both hinges were cut.

Joe used the blade to pry the hinge side of the door inward a couple of inches. Then he shoved the broken sword under his belt. He and Frank grasped the edge of the door with both hands. They gave a strong pull, then stepped aside to let it crash inward.

It hit with a loud plop. Instantly a cloud of dust filled the air, half blinding the boys. They stumbled out, but were unable to see where they were. The air, however, smelled fresh.

Frank and Joe coughed and wiped their tearing eyes. Finally they could see. To their utter amazement, they realized that they were in Vincent Steele's cellar museum!

CHAPTER XVIII

Cool Steele

FRANK led the way up the stairs. The door at the top was unlocked. Quietly they stepped out into the central hall, where lights shone from the living room.

Tiptoeing on the soft carpet, they peered into the front room of the house. Two lamps were burning, but no one was there.

"We'll have to be careful," Frank said. "Looks as if nobody's down here. Let's go upstairs."

They searched the whole house. It was empty. Returning from the second floor, the Hardys went into the kitchen, where they washed the dirt from their hands.

"Let's take a good look at that saber," Frank suggested.

They had just begun to examine the blade when a car turned into the driveway, its headlights shining through the windows.

The boys peered out the rear door. By the light reflected from the garage, they could see Vincent Steele and his wife emerge from the car. She waited while he opened the garage door and drove the car inside.

"Shall we leave by the front way?" Joe asked.

"We can handle Steele," Frank said. "Let's see what he has to say about our kidnapping. But we'd better get that saber out of sight."

Taking it from his brother, Frank tucked the blade beneath his shirt and down under his belt.

Vincent Steele opened the back door, then let his wife precede him into the house. She did not notice the boys on either side of the doorway as she walked by. When the writer entered and closed the door behind him, Frank and Joe grabbed him.

"What's this?" Steele cried out and struggled to get free.

Wheeling around, Mrs. Steele let out a long keening wail. Her husband gave up his efforts and stood as though transfixed. Staring at her, he shouted, "For goodness' sake, be quiet!"

She stopped as abruptly as she had begun. There was a long moment of silence. Then the woman said in a high voice, "I knew all along these boys were thieves and weren't really Fenton Hardy's sons. I should have let the sheriff's men take them in!"

"We're not thieves," Frank said. "And we are Fenton Hardy's sons."

"Then why did you break in here while we weren't home?" she demanded.

"We didn't," Joe told her. "We were kidnapped and brought here."

After staring at them for a moment, Mrs. Steele said, "I don't believe that!" She strode into the central hallway and picked up the phone.

"Wait a minute!" her husband called after her. "Let's find out what this is all about before you go calling the sheriff again."

Mrs. Steele hesitated, then hung up the phone. She came back to the kitchen.

"What do you boys want here?" she inquired.

In a grim tone Frank said, "We want to know why we were kidnapped and locked in that storeroom in your cellar!"

Steele stirred. "Do you mind letting me go while we discuss this? I assure you I won't run away."

Frank and Joe released their grips on the screenwriter's arms, but watched him closely.

Fastidiously brushing both coat sleeves where he had been touched, Steele said, "Now what was that about kidnapping?"

"Two men captured us at Carson's Ski Lodge," Joe said. "You must have been in on it, or they wouldn't have brought us to your house!"

"I know nothing whatever about it," Steele stated indignantly. "And I haven't the slightest idea why you were brought here."

"How could they get us in without your knowing?" Frank asked. "We must have been carried through the house. Unless your cellar has a secret entrance. Has it?"

"Not that I know of."

"Who else has seen that cave in the cellar?" Joe asked.

Steele shrugged. "As I told you before, it's supposed to be a storeroom, but we've never used it. If the cellar has a secret entrance, I would like to find out about it too. Suppose we all go down there and search for one?"

Was this a trap? Joe wondered. He looked searchingly at Frank, who nodded imperceptibly.

"Okay, Mr. Steele," he said. "But you'd better go first. Your wife, too."

"You don't trust me," Steele said flatly.

"No," Frank replied.

They descended in single file, the Steeles first, then Frank, with Joe bringing up the rear.

Downstairs, the writer frowned when he saw that the oaken door was lying on the floor with its hinges cut.

Noting his expression, Frank said, "Sorry about that, but we had no choice."

"What did you cut them with?" Steele asked.

"A knife," Frank said vaguely.

The four of them searched the cellar thoroughly. They found no evidence of any secret way into it.

"We've both been gone all evening," Steele declared. "If you were brought in through the house, your kidnappers must have picked the lock. They had no permission from us to enter the place."

"The back door was open," Mrs. Steele reminded her husband. "We don't usually lock it."

"I still don't see why anyone would use the house of an innocent person," Joe declared.

Steele shrugged. "It's an ancient building. Many people could know about the storeroom. Perhaps they figured we wouldn't have discovered you there until long after you had died of starvation."

Mrs. Steele shuddered. "How awful!"

Joe said, "Frank, I guess we'll have to presume that they're innocent, since we can't prove otherwise. Let's get out of here."

In a courteous voice Steele said, "You don't have any transportation. I'll drive you wherever you want to go."

"Thanks, but we'll call a cab," Frank said.

They started up the stairs in the same order that they had descended, Mrs. Steele in the lead. Halfway up, Frank felt the blade under his belt begin to slip. He made an attempt to hold it, but it was too late. It dropped down his pants leg and clanged against the stone step.

Vincent Steele turned quickly and picked up the broken sword. His wife looked over his shoulder.

"What in the world is this?" she asked in astonishment. "Where did it come from?"

"Under my belt," Frank said.

"You mean you had it all the time? Or did you find it in the cellar?"

"It was buried in your so-called storeroom," Joe said. "We found it while trying to dig our way out."

"Then it belongs to us," the woman declared.

Her husband interceded. "My dear, I think the law on treasure trove says that it belongs to the finder. But let's take a look at it in a better light before we all get excited."

They continued into the kitchen, where the writer examined the blade under a strong light. After turning it over and over, he shrugged and handed it back to Frank.

"It isn't worth arguing about," he said. "What good is half a sword?"

Frank said, "It's worth something to us. Our teacher may be able to use it in his magazine article."

"Yes," Joe agreed. "I'm sure he'll be interested in it. May we use your phone to call a taxi?"

When the cab came Steele accompanied the boys outside. He gave them a cordial good-by and apologized for their having been locked up in his house. Again he disclaimed any knowledge of how they got there.

The taxi pulled away. Frank told the driver to take them to the Northside Plaza Motel in Stockton.

Joe said, "Did it strike you as strange that Steele gave up the sword so easily? He must have known what it was!"

"What choice did he have?" Frank said. "We were two to one. He knew that if he didn't give it up voluntarily, we could take it away from him."

"No doubt he's in with Homer and that bunch," Joe said. "But what on earth would he have to do with the spectrograph gang?"

Frank shrugged. "It's a puzzle all right."

When they arrived at the motel, they learned that Mr. and Mrs. Hardy were in Room 103. They knocked and their mother opened the door.

"Frank! Joe!" she exclaimed with relief. "I'm so glad you're safe! How did you get away from those kidnappers?" She put an arm around each boy. "Come inside and tell me all about it."

The boys told her briefly what had happened, and showed her the broken saber. Then Frank asked how she had known about the kidnapping.

"Dad phoned from the sheriff's office. He and

Chet are out with the deputies and city police searching for you two."

"Then they escaped from that goon who took them in the car!" Frank exclaimed.

"Yes," Mrs. Hardy replied and told how Chet had outwitted their captor.

"We'd better call and let the police know we're safe," Joe said.

"I'll do it right now," Mrs. Hardy offered.

While she was on the phone, Frank and Joe wiped the blade with a soft cloth and examined it closely. They held it under the light and slanted it at various angles.

Frank shook his head. "No wonder Steele let us have this without a struggle. There's no will inscribed on this blade!"

CHAPTER XIX

Shadowy Figures

Mrs. Hardy hung up the phone and said, "Your father and Chet are out in a patrol car. The sergeant I talked to said he would inform them by radio that you're safe."

"Good," Frank said. "But I don't think we should wait for them to get back here. I'm sure Steele is in with the thugs who captured us. Chances are he's called them to his house for a conference. Joe and I'll go back there to listen in."

"We could use one of Dad's bugs for that," Joe said. "Did he bring any with him, Mom?"

"He always does, no matter where he goes," Mrs. Hardy replied. "I'll check his suitcase."

She found two small metal disks about the size of shirt buttons which could be clipped onto window drapes or to the backs of upholstered furniture. The receiver was a small, oblong box about the size of a pocket transistor radio, and had a retractable antenna. When one of the tiny microphones was placed in a room, the metal ear would pick up all conversation and broadcast it to the receiver.

Putting the device in his pocket, Joe said, "We'll have to take your car, Mom, because Dad and Chet have ours."

"All right," Mrs. Hardy said. "But be careful. If Mr. Steele is part of the gang, prowling around his house could be dangerous."

She gave Frank the keys to the Plymouth. They placed the guard end of the saber in the closet and left.

It was close to ten o'clock when the boys neared the Steeles' house. They parked a block away and walked the rest of the distance.

The front gate was locked. Frank was reaching for the split-rail fence when Joe stopped him. "Suppose Steele lied about disconnecting the electricity?"

"We'd better check," Frank agreed. "Give me the receiver for the listening device."

Joe handed him the small box. His brother extended the antenna to its full length of about three feet, then unscrewed it from the box. Setting one end on the ground, he dropped the other end against the fence.

A blue spark crackled along the narrow steel

tube. Frank kicked the antenna away from the fence and screwed it back into the receiver.

"Well," Joe said, taking the box and putting it back in his pocket, "what now?"

"We hurdle the fence," Frank decided.

Backing up, he ran toward it and cleared it like a track hurdler. Joe followed suit. Silently they crossed the lawn to the large picture window. The drapes were drawn, but not completely closed. Frank and Joe peered in. The living room was empty.

Joe opened the window, reached in, and clipped one of the tiny microphones to the back of one of the drapes.

He had barely pulled the window down when Mr. and Mrs. Steele entered the room. The boys faded around the corner of the house to the back.

A light burned in the kitchen, but shades were drawn over both the window and the glass pane in the back door. Frank tried the door and found it unlocked. Inching the door open, he peered in. No one was in sight.

"Give me the other mike," he said to Joe.

Joe handed it to him and Frank went inside. He clipped the disk under a kitchen curtain and slipped out again.

The boys retreated behind the garage. Joe flicked on the switch of the receiver. Both put their ears close to it.

Mrs. Steele's voice came through. "If your

friends are coming here tonight, I'm going to my sister's. I can't stand them."

Vincent Steele said patiently, "They're not friends, merely business associates. And they won't be staying long."

"Even five minutes is too long to suit me," his wife replied sharply. "When they arrive, I leave!"

Just then five shadowy figures moved past the garage. Obviously the other gate was not electrified. It was too dark to see the men's features. They entered the house by the back door. A few moments later the door opened again, then slammed shut. Mrs. Steele went straight to the garage and drove off.

The voices from inside the house came over the bug distinctly. Someone with an Italian accent said, "Why didn't you keep the blade, once you had your hands on it?"

"There were two of them," Steele replied. "Besides, I examined it carefully. There was no will inscribed on it!"

"Then it can't be the Adalante," a familiar voice spoke up.

Joe whispered, "I think that's Charlie."

"Right," Frank replied. "Listen."

"Yes, it is the Adalante," Steele insisted. "The letters A-N-T-E were clearly visible. But there was nothing else."

"Why did you let them escape from the cellar?" Homer asked.

"Me?" Steele said. "I wasn't even here. You locked them in. You can't seem to do anything right. First you caused poor Ettore Rossi all that trouble for nothing, because you thought he was Russo. Then you can't even lock up a couple of kids so they stay locked up!"

"Shut up!" It was Kell speaking. "You haven't done so hot either."

"I did what I was hired to do. I found the broken blade. So I'll take my payoff now."

There was a derisive laugh, then the man with the accent said, "You have not delivered the blade."

"I only agreed to locate it," Steele said. "I've done that. I walked the boys outside when they left here and got the cab's number. Then I phoned the taxi company and found out from the dispatcher that he took them to the Northside Plaza Motel in Stockton. You'll find the blade there."

The man with the accent said, "Hugo, I wish to speak to you alone. Come with me in the kitchen."

There was a short silence, then the man said in a whispering voice, "If Steele is right and there is no inscription on the saber, we could put our own on it once we get the blade!"

Hugo replied, "Not a bad idea, Hans. We could have it engraved so as to leave everything to Fabrizio Dente. Shall we pay off Steele?"

"Not until we have the sword!"

A door shut. Apparently they were returning to the others in the living room.

"I wonder who those two are," Joe said in a low voice.

"Maybe the leaders of the gang," Frank ventured.

They listened attentively, but nothing more of importance was said. Hans announced they were leaving and promised Vincent Steele he would get his money as soon as the Adalante was in their hands.

"We'll get it tomorrow," Hans said. "It should be no problem to find out which room the Hardys are in. We'll watch until they leave, then break in and steal the blade."

The five men left by the back door. Joe switched off the receiver and the boys slipped around the corner to the far side of the garage until the shadowy quintet had gone past them and into the alley.

As the back gate clicked behind them, Frank and Joe followed. A car was parked about twenty yards from the house. The men climbed in and drove away without lights. It was impossible to see the license number.

"Too bad we couldn't get a look at their faces," Joe said.

"Yes," Frank agreed. "But we still learned a lot. Now back to the motel and report to Dad."

"Okay," Joe said. "But let's stop at Swanson's and pick up some hamburgers. I'm hungry."

"All right," Frank consented.

They left by the driveway gate and made their way back to where they had parked the car. It was nearly midnight when Frank pulled into the drive-in restaurant and gave their order. As they were waiting, a green Buick drove in next to them.

Both boys turned to look. "Well, well," Frank said. "If it isn't our buddy Harry Madsen!"

"Are you guys still hanging around here?" Madsen snarled.

"Have you been following us?" Frank demanded.

"None of your business," the bulldozer operator snapped. "You'd better just watch your step."

The carhop came with their sack of hamburgers. Joe paid and Frank started the car.

As they backed out, Madsen called after them, "Remember what I said! Watch out!"

The boys did not reply and Frank drove toward the Northside Plaza.

"You think he's in with that mob?" Joe asked.

"I don't know. He could have stayed outside Steele's house tonight and kept watch, then followed us here."

Joe thought about this for a moment, then said, "I doubt it. If he was tailing us, why did he make himself known?"

"True, too."

As they neared the motel, they saw the blinking red lights of three police cars parked in front.

"Holy Toledo!" Joe exclaimed. "More trouble!"

Frank parked the car in front of their parents' room. Three policemen were standing there, guarding the door!

CHAPTER XX

Duel in the Dumps

"WE'RE Mr. Hardy's sons," Frank said to the patrolmen. "What happened?"

"Your father can tell you," one of the officers replied. "He's inside."

They found the motel room crowded with people—Mr. and Mrs. Hardy, Chet, two more policemen and four handcuffed prisoners.

Frank and Joe identified Charlie, Homer, Kell and the fake Signor Zonko, mastermind of the Bayport bank robbery.

"His real name is Hugo Hausner," Mr. Hardy said. "He's a Swiss citizen and an international thief, according to the police here."

"How did you catch them?" Joe asked.

"Chet and I arrived just after five of them entered to steal the sword Adalante," Mr. Hardy replied. "We rushed in when we heard your mother scream. I knocked out Charlie with a karate chop. Chet got Homer with an uppercut and your mother banged Kell on the head with the telephone. Then Chet and I subdued Hausner. Unfortunately, in all the confusion, the fifth man escaped taking the broken blade."

"We'll catch up with him," one of the officers declared. "From your description, he must be Hugo's brother Hans. He's got an Italian accent. Hugo sometimes speaks with an accent, too, but his is phony. We've put out an all-points bulletin on Hans."

The other policeman said, "Let's get these guys down to headquarters. Maybe one of them will talk."

The suspects were hustled into a police car. Mr. Hardy and the three boys followed in the Plymouth. Mrs. Hardy remained at the motel.

At headquarters the bank robbers were informed of their legal rights to consult a lawyer, then were put in separate cells. It was not long before Charlie agreed to turn informer in return for a recommendation of leniency when he came to trial.

"Hans Hausner came to the States because some guy in Switzerland had hired him to locate the guard end of the sword Adalante," Charlie began. "Also, he was supposed to prevent Ettore Russo from going to Tessin to claim his grandfather's estate."

Joe said, "But Hans chased the wrong man at first!"

"Right. Then a publicity story on Ettore Rossi appeared in the newspaper and pointed out the similarity in names," Charlie said. "So he realized his mistake."

"What about Hugo Hausner?" Frank asked.

"He pulled a number of bank robberies. The last one was in Bayport. Somehow his voice was taped, so he cut out. Came to the Coast and worked with Hans."

"And how does Steele fit into all this?" Mr. Hardy inquired.

Charlie said Hans had contacted the writer to help him locate the sword because Steele knew a lot about the area that had once been Russo's vineyard. Steele agreed, for a price, to try to find the blade.

Charlie added, "I understand Steele's wife didn't know anything about this."

The story continued to unfold. After the Bayport robbery, Red Bowes was ordered to shadow the Hardys. Two more of Hugo's men had gone to Chicago, where they successfully shook down a top racketeer for a large sum by selling him his own voiceprint from Mr. Hardy's file. From there they had continued on to New Orleans for the same reason.

Homer, Charlie, and Kell had come to San

Francisco to work on gang boss Rocky Morgan. But instead of paying off, Morgan had sent his gang after them, with the resulting gunfight in Chinatown.

"Do you know anything about the three hundred thousand dollars the gang stole in Bayport?" Mr. Hardy asked.

"That's hidden at our motel, the Sundance," Charlie replied.

A police team was dispatched immediately to recover the loot.

"What do you know about Harry Madsen?" Frank asked.

"Who?" Charlie looked blank. "Never heard of him."

When the boys explained to the police who Madsen was, they decided to bring the bulldozer operator in for questioning. But since it was now long past midnight, they agreed to wait until the morning.

Mr. Hardy and the three boys drove back to the Northside Plaza, where the boys picked up their rented Chevrolet and headed for their own motel. It was not until they were almost there that Joe remembered something.

"Hey!" he said. "That sack of hamburgers we bought is still in the Plymouth!"

"You forgot our food?" Chet said in an outraged voice. "And I haven't eaten since dinnertime!"

"Forget it," Frank told him. "Unless you like cold hamburgers!"

Next morning the trio was up early.

"Let's drive to the Northside Plaza and have breakfast with Mom and Dad," Frank suggested.

"Good thought," Chet agreed.

As soon as they were seated in the motel restaurant, Mr. Hardy reported that he had already talked to the police by telephone.

"Steele has been arrested for allowing his property to be used by kidnappers," he said. "Also they questioned Madsen but released him."

"They should have held him for attempted murder!" Joe said, eyes blazing.

"Well, he had no connection with the Hausner gang. He was merely teed off because you beat him at fencing," Mr. Hardy replied.

"Didn't he put the rattler in our car?" Joe demanded.

"He did. But it was not venomous because its poison sacs had been removed," Mr. Hardy replied. "He just wanted to scare you. He told us where he got the snake and the police checked out his story."

"And he shorted our horn and called Mrs. Steele telling her we were thieves, right?" Frank said.

"Yes."

"I just love that guy!" Joe grumbled.

"We ran into him a couple of times at the

drive-in restaurant and last night he told us to watch our step!" Frank said.

"That was coincidence," Mr. Hardy stated. "He stops there for a sandwich now and then, and the threat was just talk."

"Did he phone our motel one time and tell us to get out of the state?" Joe asked.

Mr. Hardy nodded. "But he was not the one who called you at the Steeles' house."

"Then who was it?" Frank wanted to know.

"Hugo Hausner. I found out from Chief Collig. He had the voiceprint you sent him checked against the ones you made in Bayport. Mr. Dollinger let him have the whole set. It matched Hausner's."

Mr. Hardy went on to say that the police had also informed him that his voiceprint file, minus the two spectrograms that had been peddled in Chicago and New Orleans, had been recovered from the gang's motel. The Bayport bank loot had been found there intact, too. Hugo Hausner's two hoods who had sold the spectrographs were arrested in New Orleans.

"There will be a good-sized reward for recovering the bank money," Fenton Hardy said. "And you boys are entitled to most of it."

After breakfast they discussed the problem of the missing Hans Hausner. The police had not found a trace of him yet. Suddenly Joe recalled something.

"Frank, remember when Hans took Hugo into the Steele kitchen for a private talk? He said once they got hold of the blade, they could have a will engraved on it!"

"Of course!" Frank exclaimed. "If we check local engravers in the classified telephone directory, we might get a lead on him!"

Quickly they made a list from the yellow pages of places where engraving was done in the Stockton area. Then they divided the list, Mr. Hardy and Chet taking half, Frank and Joe taking the rest. They agreed to meet again at the motel around noon.

The Hardy boys went to engraver after engraver with no luck. At eleven o'clock, with only a couple of places remaining on their list, they entered a small jewelry store.

When they told the middle-aged proprietor who they were and what they wanted, he said, "A man with an Italian accent? Why, you just missed him. He left no more than a minute ago, as soon as I finished the work. He had me inscribe on a broken blade that the Russo fortune would go to somebody named Fabrizio Dente."

"Which way did he go?" Joe asked eagerly.

"He said he wanted to catch a noon plane, so I imagine he headed for the airport. I noticed him getting into a dark sedan parked out front."

"Thank you," Frank said. "Let's get moving, Joe."

Joe took the wheel of the Chevy, started the engine, and shot away from the curb. He took the most direct route to the airport, reasoning that Hausner, who had plenty of time before his plane took off, would not be hurrying. The boys spotted the dark sedan halfway to the airport.

"That's his car," Frank said. "I recognize it. The one they used to transport us to Steele's after the kidnapping."

"Right," Joe said and poured on the gas.

The fugitive gave a startled look when the Hardys' car pulled up alongside of him. Joe slowed, cut in, and forced the sedan off the road onto the shoulder. Hausner panicked.

He jumped out and started to run across the city dump which stretched to the right. Frank and Joe took after him, scrambling across mountains of trash. They gained steadily.

"Hausner! You can't get away!" Frank called out.

The fugitive turned his head to utter an oath, but kept climbing over the mounds of debris.

The gap narrowed with each step, however. Now Hausner's labored breathing could be heard by his pursuers.

"Halt! Stop!" Joe cried. The Swiss was nearly in his grasp.

Hausner spun around. In his right hand he held the broken saber, with which he lashed furiously at Joe while making guttural noises.

Frank spied a stripped umbrella lying in the junk. He picked it up and leaped in front of Joe, brandishing the handle like a sword.

The Swiss turned and slashed at him with the saber. Nimbly skipping aside, Frank thrust and lunged. Hausner let out a grunt as the tip of the umbrella poked him in the stomach. Then Frank cracked the umbrella frame across Hausner's wrist and knocked the saber from his hand.

Frank and Joe subdued their quarry without any further resistance. After they turned him over to the police, they drove back to the motel.

They found their father, mother, and Chet waiting. Quickly they told what had happened.

"Great job!" Mr. Hardy praised his sons. "Now let's have a look at that saber."

He examined the hilt under a powerful magnifying glass. Nothing besides the letters A-N-T-E and the inscription was on either side of the stubby blade.

"Can I see it, Dad?" Frank asked. He studied the hand guard carefully. It had a leather protective lining. Frank pulled it out. Nothing was hidden beneath it.

Suddenly Joe said, "Hey, what's that?"

"Where?" Frank asked.

"Something's written on the underside of that piece of leather."

Frank examined it. "It's the will! Dad, we've found it!"

Mr. Hardy took a close look. "It sure is," he confirmed. He read the tiny inscription. It left three-fourths of Russo's fortune to his first grandson.

"That's Ettore Russo!" Chet exclaimed. "We've solved our case!"

The boys sent a cable to the fencing master, telling him the good news. They included the information that Mr. and Mrs. Hardy would personally deliver the saber to Russo in Bellinzona, Switzerland.

"You haven't finished your vacation," Frank said to his parents. "This way you can tour Switzerland."

Mr. Hardy smiled. "We might just do that!"

"There's still one loose end that bothers me," Joe said. "I wonder if it was June Fall who tore those pages from the book about Giovanni Russo."

"Why don't you phone the college library and ask if they know the pages are missing?" Mr. Hardy suggested. "Now that the big mystery is solved, you've got plenty of time."

Joe went to the telephone, little knowing that more excitement would soon come their way in *The Flickering Torch Mystery*. When he had finished the call, he grinned.

"Guess what?" he said. "Those pages have been missing for three years!"

Join Frank and Joe in a new PC adventure game!
Nancy Drew: Last Train to Blue Moon Canyon
The Hardy Boys® and their sleuthing pal, Nancy Drew®, are invited to a mystery-solving party on an elegant private train. Climb aboard to interrogate suspects, search for clues and unravel secrets in this thrilling mystery adventure game!
Don't dare miss this train!
Go to www.HerInteractive.com or call 1-800-461-8787 to order. Available in stores now!
NEW! FEATURING THE HARDY BOYS!
NANCY DREW
Last Train to Blue Moon Canyon
#1 PC Adventure Game Series in America!
Collect all the award-winning Nancy Drew mystery games
PC CD-ROM SOFTWARE
FOR MYSTERY FANS 10 TO ADULT
Nancy Drew and The Hardy Boys are registered trademarks of Simon & Schuster, Inc.
Created by
HeR Interactive

Match Wits with The Hardy Boys®!

Collect the Complete **Hardy Boys Mystery Stories®**

by Franklin W. Dixon

#1: The Tower Treasure
#2: The House on the Cliff
#3: The Secret of the Old Mill
#4: The Missing Chums
#5: Hunting for Hidden Gold
#6: The Shore Road Mystery
#7: The Secret of the Caves
#8: The Mystery of Cabin Island
#9: The Great Airport Mystery
#10: What Happened at Midnight
#11: While the Clock Ticked
#12: Footprints Under the Window
#13: The Mark on the Door
#14: The Hidden Harbor Mystery
#15: The Sinister Signpost
#16: A Figure in Hiding
#17: The Secret Warning
#18: The Twisted Claw
#19: The Disappearing Floor
#20: The Mystery of the Flying Express
#21: The Clue of the Broken Blade
#22: The Flickering Torch Mystery
#23: The Melted Coins
#24: The Short-Wave Mystery
#25: The Secret Panel
#26: The Phantom Freighter
#27: The Secret of Skull Mountain
#28: The Sign of the Crooked Arrow
#29: The Secret of the Lost Tunnel
#30: The Wailing Siren Mystery
#31: The Secret of Wildcat Swamp
#32: The Crisscross Shadow
#33: The Yellow Feather Mystery
#34: The Hooded Hawk Mystery
#35: The Clue in the Embers
#36: The Secret of Pirates' Hill
#37: The Ghost at Skeleton Rock
#38: The Mystery at Devil's Paw
#39: The Mystery of the Chinese Junk
#40: Mystery of the Desert Giant
#41: The Clue of the Screeching Owl
#42: The Viking Symbol Mystery
#43: The Mystery of the Aztec Warrior
#44: The Haunted Fort
#45: The Mystery of the Spiral Bridge
#46: The Secret Agent on Flight 101
#47: Mystery of the Whale Tattoo
#48: The Arctic Patrol Mystery
#49: The Bombay Boomerang
#50: Danger on Vampire Trail
#51: The Masked Monkey
#52: The Shattered Helmet
#53: The Clue of the Hissing Serpent
#54: The Mysterious Caravan
#55: The Witchmaster's Key
#56: The Jungle Pyramid
#57: The Firebird Rocket
#58: The Sting of the Scorpion
#59: Night of the Werewolf
#60: Mystery of the Samurai Sword
#61: The Pentagon Spy
#62: The Apeman's Secret
#63: The Mummy Case
#64: Mystery of Smugglers Cove
#65: The Stone Idol
#66: The Vanishing Thieves

The Hardy Boys Back-to-Back
#1: The Tower Treasure/#2: The House on the Cliff

Celebrate over 70 Years with the World's Greatest Super Sleuths!